LOVE IS A SOLITARY GAME

Esther Tusquets

LOVE IS A
SOLITARY GAME

Translated by Bruce Penman

JOHN CALDER · LONDON
RIVERRUN PRESS · NEW YORK

First published in Great Britain in 1985 by
John Calder (Publishers) Limited
18 Brewer Street, London W1R 4AS

And in the United States of America by
Riverrun Press Inc
1170 Broadway,
New York, NY 10001

Originally published in Spanish as *Elamores un juego solitalo*
in 1979 by Editorial Lumen, Barcelona

British Library Cataloguing in Publication Data

Tusquets, Esther
  Love is a solitary game.
  I. Title   II. El amor es un juego solitario.
  English
  863'.64 F   PQ6670.U8

  ISBN 0-7145-4042-0

Library of Congress Cataloging in Publication Data

Tusquets, Esther
  Love is a solitary game.

  Translation of: Amor es un juego solitario.
  I. Title.
PQ6670.U8A413 1985   863'64   85-10878
ISBN 0-7145-4042-0 (pbk.)

Photoset in 11 on 13 pt Baskerville by Alan Sutton Publishing Ltd
Printed in Great Britain by Redwood Burn Ltd, Trowbridge

A mysterious message goes out ... a strange perfume invades the springtime forest, and the great apes uneasily seek out the dens of their mates. The perfume tastes of dust — a fine, slightly bitter dust that dries the lips and clings to the roof of the mouth; it causes a curious, slack lassitude, imposing a strange rhythm, a special tempo like that of a slow-motion film, on the movements of the apes, as they snuff the air with dilated nostrils and wander through the woods with the heavy, sluggish motions of a pantomime. The perfume has an unmistakable quality, like the scent of fleshy, baneful flowers such as those exquisitely beautiful tree-orchids which decompose so rapidly into an evil slush. It recalls the smell of incipient putrefaction, of the floor of a circus at the end of a performance, after the triumphant parade of the animals, the smell of houses that have been shut up for many months, or of dens sealed off by impalpable walls of silence. It is a poisonous, bitter-sweet odour.

'See what Elia's reading!'

'It's just an adventure story,' said Elia.

'Adventures, eh!' said the boy; he whisked the book out of her hands and began to read it aloud. (Had Elia always hated reading aloud, or did she begin to hate it from that moment?) Surrounded by his circle of friends, the boy read out the passage about the forest in springtime and the apes, with much comic emphasis, stressing or ridiculing every other word.

Elia realised that this passage did not really make much sense within the general context of the story into which it had been inserted. She wondered what humorous or perverse caprice had moved the author — could it be a private game to relieve the monotony of turning out a weekly or monthly series of stories that differed only in outward circumstances while pitilessly repeating the same plot? — what perverse caprice had prompted the author to bring it in at this particular point . . . the great apes with their feverish eyes and their dilated nostrils, snuffing the air and wandering restlessly through the forest as they track down the heavy scent which the females suddenly begin to emit every spring as they come into season; while the females themselves lie huddled in passionate yearning in the depths of their lairs, perhaps alarmed by their own odour, which announces the beginning of a period of passive expectation.

Elia hadn't noticed it before — she had passed over those words, those few lines, without special attention, being solely interested in the successive adventures of the hero in the story, who was lost in the densest and most tangled part of the jungle — but now her eyes were opened by the meaning manner in which the boy was reading her book, by the stress he laid upon certain words (not all of which were familiar to her), and above all by the spiteful attention with which the other children were listening, by their pursed lips and flushed cheeks. They were looking at her (not for the first time) with eyes dark and ugly with mistrust and suspicion, looking at her as at someone outside their group, at someone who couldn't be fully accepted and who was fated always to wander on the fringe of their closed summer holiday world, because the boys were listening to the passage about the

6

springtime forest and the apes in rut while the girls pretended to be shocked and put on a show of not listening; and the book was (naturally) one that Elia was reading. Boys and girls alike couldn't help remembering once again that Elia's parents didn't go to church on Sundays. And no one believed, much as they would have liked to, that this was because their car had broken down; even Elia didn't maintain that thesis with conviction, and anyway the church wasn't far enough away to provide them with a dispensation from going on foot, in terms of the monolithic religious structure of Spain in the 1950s, which measured and quantified everything. Nor must it be forgotten that Elia's parents are apparently on the point of separating, and that they are often visited at the weekend by friends of the arty and eccentric type (to quote the words used by the other children's parents, in a superior voice and as if to avoid saying something worse), with whom they drink and joke and listen to music all night until dawn. It is even whispered in the hotel — and the children know about it — that some mornings, just as the blood-red sun rises out of the waveless sea, Elia's parents have gone swimming naked with their friends on one of the neighbouring beaches, without bothering very much whether or not they were concealed from the astonished and scandalised gaze of the hotel waiters and chambermaids, or from the gaze of the boys, some of whom got out of their bedrooms one night to go and watch them from behind the bushes. The children also remember in the same instant (it all comes to them at once in a single disquieting syndrome) that Elia has always been allowed — ever since they've known her, at least, ever since they started coming regularly to this particular coastal resort for the summer holidays — to go for long walks in the woods by herself, or to take a rowing-boat out with some boy or other, and go out to a distance where she couldn't be followed by vigilant parental

7

eyes — the eyes of the other children's parents, that is to say, since her own father and mother were probably up in their room, or if they had got down to the beach they never showed much interest in the comings and goings of their daughter. The children in that summer hotel of the 1950s were not at all surprised to find that this strange girl, whom they had never fully accepted, should read books which appeared to be harmless tales of adventure like the ones they sometimes read themselves but which contained terrible passages such as were never found in the books their own parents bought them — insidious, perverse passages about the jungle in springtime.

Many years later, Elia laughed as she remembered the distrust and suspicion of those children in the hotel and on the beach, and of other children at school and at home. Had they after all done her harm or good by keeping her on the fringe of their groups, with strictly limited rights of access to the interior? Anyway, those kids and their parents were quite right about me, she thought, time has shown how right they were. All that I am today follows in a direct, unbroken line — essentially unbroken even in the first years of my marriage — from my unrestricted reading; from the impending separation of my parents which never actually happened; from my parents' friends who bathed naked with them and drank a bit too much, and even went so far as not to go to church on Sundays in the middle of the 1950s, without so much as pretending that their car had broken down: it follows from those long lonely walks and bicycle rides with a piece of bread, a slab of chocolate and a book in my handbag or carrier-basket, and from those first intimate contacts, bold or furtive, in the boat, in the fresh air and the sunshine, out at sea, far from adult eyes . . .

After forgetting about it for all these years, Elia now remembers the scandalous passage which had been introduced in so unsuitable and unjustifiable a manner into a children's adventure story: and it occurs to her that spring is here again — another spring has come — and that the great apes, gorillas perhaps or orang-utangs, are snuffing the air in their remote forests, uneasily ready to begin the same ritual dance around the dens of the females, amid a mixed aroma of sex, dust and flowers. "A dark summons, a deep-felt summons . . ." Elia recalls, and she laughs. Male and female are brought together from distant parts of the forest by a mysterious and unknown olfactory affinity; with the arrival of spring and the mating season, each female releases a unique, unmistakable odour, and this odour is picked up on the other side of the forest by the male — the very male who chooses that particular female and is destined to be her mate — and the two of them at once begin to seek each other out, over a distance of many miles, without hesitation and without impatience, because each knows with total certainty that the other exists, transmitting the aroma or receiving it. Both are in the grip of a common desire which will bring them together to couple amid the exultant orchids of the jungle in springtime.

Elia laughs again at the memory of the reception of this episode, with its saccharine, ambiguous style, popping up unexpectedly in the middle of an adventure story; the ambiguity may in fact have increased its effect, to judge by the expressions on the faces of the other children. It also crosses her mind that there is a remarkable amount of common ground between that far-off scene and the springtime which now surrounds her: an obscure interweaving of inexorable, well-aimed instincts, a host of females unconsciously emitting a bitter-sweet aroma and of males searching for them uneasily, slowly and greedily through

9

the blossoming forests. The picture evoked was full of inconsistencies: the few lines in which it was described were basically absurd and indeed ludicrous, so that only children of the Spanish bourgeoisie in the fifties could have found them smutty or erotic; and yet it was as if they were taking on a new meaning — itself necessarily absurd and faintly ludicrous. And the fact is that the first signals were so weak as to be almost imperceptible: no more than a slight uneasiness at hearing a certain name, which Clara had often mentioned over quite a long period, though always with complete indifference, or in terms of mockery or disdain. Yet suddenly one day, or over a long series of days, that name began to disturb her more and more. Or the signal might take the form of an inexplicable and inopportune feeling of interest which suddenly overcame her in the course of a tedious conversation, in which she was hardly participating and to which she contributed only with polite monosyllables; when that name cropped up it always took her by surprise, although she could not understand why she should be surprised by the fact that people were talking about the owner of the name in a city where there are so few things to discuss and where almost every conversation ends in gossip. This applied to any anecdote or reference or comment which had any bearing on the owner of the name (the male ape who was already observing Elia, although she was not yet aware of the fact, through the blossoming springtime of the city). In the most boring circumstances, she felt sudden, instantaneous flashes of curiosity, which led her to ask pointless questions about him, much to Clara's astonishment (if Clara was among those present). Elia herself did not know what was happening, because the distant call is very weak and unsubstantial in its early stages, like an underground rumbling which hardly reaches the surface and can scarcely be heard amid the bustle of our conscious life.

10

But one day Clara, apparently much amused though also unmistakably embarrassed, brought her a definite communication from the male ape, who had unquestionably chosen Clara as his messenger. Then Elia definitely knew that there really was someone there at the other end of the strong and secret chord of instinct — a living creature in his den thinking of her in hers, a male ape who had carefully absorbed the odour of a particular female and distinguished it from the countless other aromas of springtime, from the odours of countless other available females. He had chosen her, and was now on her track in a strange, ecstatic yet unhurried pursuit.

Elia was disturbed by the fact that she did not even know what her admirer looked like, though she must have seen him at one time or another. Clara said that he had even been in Elia's house on one occasion (though he had been struck dumb by the passion he felt for his hostess and the terror he felt for her cats), and that they had both been present at the same festivity quite recently. Elia must have heard him speak at one time or another, too, but she could not remember what he said or the tone of his voice. It was strange that this unknown should have chosen her, distinguishing her from all the other available but rejected females, and that he should now be stubbornly thinking about her in his native habitat, his den, while Elia still did not know him, and could not even imagine what he was like. It was disturbing that he should have fallen into so extraordinary a folly, such a total loss of contact with reality — the reality, that is, of ordinary social existence. Perhaps that is why Elia had to summon up memories of her childhood reading and try to place him in an alternative reality based on apes and jungles. Anyway, he had apparently appointed her to be his initiator . . . he would entrust himself to her care, and she, with the aid of the Divine mercy, would accept this fervent, docile and obedient

11

apprentice, and be his teacher. This, or something very like it, was the message transmitted by Clara. Unable to control her laughter, but blushing in acute embarrassment, she had stammered:

"He says that only you . . . that only with you . . ."

Elia also laughed, but was surprised to discover that she was inwardly flattered and secretly disturbed by this incredible proposition.

"What nonsense!" she said "why he doesn't even know me."

"Yes he does. He's even been in your house, with a lot of other people, admittedly, and you took no notice of him, and didn't even look at him, but he was there and saw you and decided at once that with you he would find the courage . . . that it would have to be with you or not at all."

"What nonsense!" said Elia, laughing again, and Clara laughed too. She had got over the embarrassment of passing the message, and had stopped blushing; a faint apprehension, a slight twinge of fear, had perhaps been calmed by Elia's last words. But Elia herself was conscious of something stirring in her inmost feelings: amid disgust, disenchantment and remote memories of childhood reading, she could not escape the thought of a certain adventure story that spoke of the aroma, or perhaps the stench, emitted by female apes in the mating season, and described (what nonsense!) how the males choose their mates before they have even met them, knowing nothing about them but their smell, and then seek them out in a tireless search through the dark forests of desire.

That message, thought Elia, was the raucous call of an ape — a bad-tempered orang-utang or a gross, hairy gorilla — that was spying on her in the springtime forests, thinking about her obsessively, with mad intensity; and indeed he could hardly be quite sane. And he had only seen her for a few moments, he could only have heard a few casual, unthinking words from her lips, probably addressed to the company in general rather than to himself. (Elia could not even remember either of the occasions when they were said to have met.) He had probably chosen her only because of her secret and shameful odour, the gentle emanation of her sex. His choice was probably based on the delirium of an overheated imagination, or possibly (the distinction is difficult to draw) of a ferociously creative imagination, capable of inventing the beloved out of practically nothing. He had chosen her in one of those frenzies to which very young people (and older people as well, thought Elia) are driven by the sheer magnitude of their loneliness, their vast, limitless, intolerably painful solitude. For this is a very young ape, as Clara has already confirmed, an uninitiated ape; a light-headed poet of an ape, who has given up the study of smutty pictures and supposedly erotic literature to devote himself to the caressing repetition of Elia's name in his room. From Clara's unflattering description, Elia imagines that room to be small, dusty and damp, full of oldish but not antique furniture, dubious in value and inconvenient in use — furniture which has to be crammed into less and less space with the passage of the years as more pieces accumulate, and perhaps also as the result of moving house to smaller and cheaper premises. It is the room of a bachelor belonging to a middle class in decline (though not yet sunken into actual poverty, where it would suffer greater physical deprivation and economic stress but might enjoy more amusement and more freedom); and a middle class in decline is often given to the joyless accumulation of such possessions, not for the pleasure of choosing, buying or owning them, but simply to avoid the pain that would be caused by the wasteful business of throwing them out, once they have established themselves for some forgotten reason as part of the household. That small,

13

overfurnished room also has too many rugs, curtains and hangings (a fad of the boy's mother, which drives him to despair) and too many books, reviews and papers piled up everywhere, even on the floor (an eccentric habit of the son, which drives his mother to distraction). The clothes that the boy has taken off are carefully folded and stacked on a chair, over the back of which his jacket is hanging; the door is carefully shut (though unfortunately it has no lock or bolt, and the boy does not like to ask his mother for one), and the light is extinguished. Elia imagines the young man — the youthful ape, the hairy gorilla, the poetic chimpanzee — thinking about her, reconstituting her image or inventing a new one for her, undressing her, calling out to her . . .

And his call crosses the urban forest, the pitiless asphalt jungle, making its way from den to den, from one bedroom to another, from bed to bed. For Elia, too, is spending long hours every day lying in slothful torpor on her bed, finding the hot spring weather oppressive and hostile, as she does every year. It is a suffocating heat, which blights the roses, magnolias and orchids at the height of their blossoming. She has a spacious bedroom, with pink wallpaper and a pink carpet. The pieces of furniture it contains are few in number and dark in colour; Elia selected them one by one, with loving care, in the various antique shops of the city . . . From the courtyard below, the voices of the local children come up through the open window; their holidays have not yet officially begun, but they seem to have time off almost all day long. Their voices are extraordinarily disturbing in the golden light of morning. The slits of the shutters are open; and, as the day wears on, parallel lines of light march inexorably across the room, and sometimes across Elia's body . . . Elia remembered certain occasions when she had lain there, fast asleep or lazily pretending to be, with a man happily watching the slow and subtle play of the rays of

14

golden light over her pearly skin, watching the warm pathway of light, the smooth, throbbing luminosity, as it slid caressingly, envelopingly onwards, creeping over her shoulders and over her breasts — she stirred and trembled at that contact — and passing on over her thighs and belly to a shadowed, moist and fleecy place which the light of day should never see; until the persistence of the man's gaze or of the golden caress of the sunlight brought her to life like Danae. In a mood of gentle happiness, she slowly emerged from her slumbers, as if wading through warm shallow water or putting aside curtains of the finest purple gauze; at first there would be something remote about her, establishing a certain distance between herself and her companion. She had to be courted all over again before the incorporeal embrace of the golden light was replaced by the bodily embraces of the man ... his hands, mouth and thighs ... On certain afternoons, she remembered, the two experiences seemed to flow together, as if one grew naturally out of the other.

Elia listens to the shouting of the children in the neighbouring courtyard. From time to time, when she does not feel too sleepy or too unwell, she gets up, puts on her dressing gown and goes and stands at the window. The children stop playing and look up towards her for a moment; they show no curiosity, and perhaps do not even see her. They do show a little more interest, in fact, when she stands at the window with her cat in her arms. Their shrill and irritant cries shatter the golden morning. Elia goes back to bed, and amuses herself by studying the play of light from the shutters over her naked body. Alternately waking and slipping back into a torpid slumber, bored with the very ideas of fulfilment, enthusiasm and pleasure — perhaps also bored with the boredom of despair itself — Elia decides not to break the circle of her own laziness and inertia during the next few days. With growing concentration, with an interest which she cannot and does not even try to explain, she thinks about the youthful ape, of whom she knows little except that he is thinking about her, wanting her as he lies in his narrow bachelor's bed. Has Clara already told him that Elia spends her mornings and part of her afternoons lying naked in bed, in a pink-white room, watching the parallel strips of light from the shutters slide over her body and listening to the shrill cries of the children in the courtyard? She knows that he wants her and is calling to her from his narrow, hard bachelor's bed, surrounded by excessive amounts of furniture, rugs and curtains, with his shoes lined up beside the bed and his clothes carefully folded on a chair. Perhaps he has been looking at certain pictures, or hiding them quickly again at the bottom of the drawer, with language exercises and unfinished poems. Perhaps he has been reading the misadventures, the wonderful deeds and the sorrows of the unfortunate Justine — there can be no doubt that he likes the works of the great marquis. This is the time when he is supposed to be taking his siesta, and he has closed the shutters and drawn the curtains, partly because he enjoys thinking about her in the shadows and partly to avoid the first suspicious glance that his mother will direct at him if she suddenly comes into the room, as she may. He is lying face down on the bed, lovingly, tenderly, caressingly repeating Elia's name, summoning up the few brief visual images of her that he carried away from a meeting which she cannot even remember, although she has tried to recall it with the help of Clara's description. He has had those images with him ever since: he sees long, white fingers with sharp, dark-red nails, straying over the body of her cat, making their way against the grain through its golden fur; he sees her unpainted lips contract into a disdainful, mocking expression, a grimace which suggests an impertinent teenager or perhaps a spoilt child; he sees the short, undulating dance of her hair when

16

she shakes her head and laughs; he sees the faint, fluttering pulse in her throat, an almost imperceptible movement which makes him long to touch the spot and feel the throb of her life under his finger tips. He retains and preserves the images like unique pieces in an exotic treasure; he caresses them in the obscurity of his bedroom; he combines them in a thousand different patterns. There is something grotesque, sad and even pathetic — and certainly something very disturbing — about the thought of that virginal, unawakened lonely organ, with no experience of other organs, other hands, other tongues . . .

Elia's inexplicable but ill-concealed curiosity about the boy had prompted a friend to tell the story about him . . . Who could it have been? — Not Clara anyway because Clara would have been too embarrassed to describe a thing like that, and anyway it wasn't a message from the ape-poet himself this time; the last thing he would have wanted would have been for the matter to be discussed and commented on in public, especially with great gusts of general laughter, and especially in front of Elia. No it was another woman, older than Clara and much more sarcastic and spiteful. "At a party one day, we were all looking at some really crazy pictures which someone had brought over from a sex-shop in London. That boy broke out into a sweat; his eyes went all glassy, his tongue stuck out between his lips, his hands grasped the edge of the table, and his body began to move backwards and forwards in a most ridiculous way. He made not the slightest attempt to hide what was going on — perhaps he didn't even realise it was happening."

Yes, thought Elia, this is an organ with no knowledge of other organs, or hands, or nipples, or tongues. On that occasion it broke out in desperate revolt, in a useless, painful assault on the rough cloth of the boy's ill-cut trousers; and even now, perhaps, it is burrowing insistently into the softness

17

of his sheets (which Elia imagines as old, cotton sheets, carefully ironed by his mother), while his hand makes its way cautiously down to his groin, and he sinks his tear-stained face more and more deeply into his pillow, as he repeats in an interminable sing-song, through clenched teeth, the short and sweet syllables of her name.

Clara again served as intermediary, though she seemed somewhat embarrassed and reluctant, as if she did not like the message she brought; which was that the ape-poet did not want to expose himself to the risk of being refused a hearing (he must be much too sensitive, thought Elia, or else much too conceited), and was therefore asking in advance for permission to ring her up. And so, one day that spring, Elia finally heard his voice at the other end of the line — a voice which even now she could not remember ever having heard before; rather a low-pitched voice, perhaps, but free from hesitation. Before long the voice was uttering what seemed to be one of those sudden, rash, indiscreet proposals which shy people are apt to make. But perhaps it was not sudden indiscretion or even an improvisation, perhaps it was an apparent indiscretion which had really been long and carefully premeditated, or even discussed at length with Clara. For Clara, despite her initial reluctance to serve as messenger, had also been playing the parts of accomplice and conspirator, for reasons which were not yet clear. Anyway, the young man asked her, choosing his words and weighing his terms with great care, if he could see her alone some time, as soon as possible, though not on Sunday morning, which was Elia's first suggestion. Ricardo — for that was the name of the ape-poet, who seemed to be rapidly losing his simian characteristics as she listened to that voice, anxious but under perfect control, at the other end of the wire — Ricardo explained that Sunday mornings had always reminded him of milky coffee and sweet buns, of everyday domesticity . . . The

18

streets of the city and the surrounding country are full of terrible married couples, carefully carrying little packets of sweets, taking their children for walks and stuffing them with toffees and chocolate; all the children are in their Sunday best, and women's hands are busy arranging mantillas and missals . . . The whole atmosphere is absolutely inadequate and unsuitable for the first meeting of a nymph and an uninitiated faun. Some other morning would be fine.

They did meet some other morning, with nothing special about it except that it was not a Sunday morning, in an empty café. The ape-like image, already weakened by the sound of his voice over the telephone, now vanished entirely; it was impossible to imagine this thin, weakly youth in any sort of forest. His hips looked too wide for the rest of his emaciated figure. His thin brown hair was combed back; it looked somewhat greasy, though that could be hair-oil or brilliantine. His eyes were colourless and watery behind his steel-rimmed spectacles. He had held out a sweaty hand to her with a decisive movement — perhaps also with the secret fear which we feel when we meet an animal which, though tame, may be dangerous — and held her soft little hand in it only a few seconds longer than the prescribed time. Then he sat on the sofa, uncomfortable in his suit (which, as Elia could now confirm, was badly cut from a harsh and ugly cloth), and did his best, by useless gestures, ineffective hissing noises and half-hearted clapping of his hands, to attract the attention of the two waiters who were talking to each other on the other side of the counter. From time to time they interrupted their conversation to look around the room with an absent gaze — an expert, chilly gaze which went straight through him without seeing him, or which passed just to one side of his body or just over his head. Elia was amused, reflecting that the subject to be initiated was not an ape-poet but an invisible poet; finally she decided to call one

19

of the waiters herself; he came over at once to take the order, went away again and came back contemptuously to put a coca-cola in front of the poet and a pot of horrible tea-bag tea in front of Elia. She was afraid for a moment that the waiter was going to open his mouth and say "May I ask, Madame, what a lady like you is doing with a boy like that?" The question would have been embarrassing, and puzzling too; for how is a woman to explain to a hostile waiter, or to anyone else for that matter, that in reality the whole thing is a question of the jungle in springtime, where the females emit a strange perfume and where a certain male (who happens to be this loutish, clumsy boy, this ugly adolescent attired in an impossible suit, with the further disadvantage of being invisible) has mysteriously picked up the aroma of her sex and has chosen her and her alone to rescue him from his invisibility and from all his fears? How, above all, is she to explain the depth of her feelings to the waiter? This is something that she has not yet been able to explain to herself since she is ready to swear that she has never before felt any particular interest in very young men. (Ricardo is certainly very young indeed and Elia is twice as old as he is; which must be why the waiter looks so shocked, why his mouth has that look of mockery and disgust . . . or are these merely the imaginings of an oversensitive woman?) Nor has it ever before occurred to Elia that there could be anything espe-cially exciting about virginity in general or even her own virginity in particular — less, much less in the virginity of a boy whom she hardly knew. So how can she explain to the waiter that on this occasion she feels profoundly disturbed, moved, stimulated and summoned to action by something which has nothing to do with love and little enough to do with desire as she has known and experienced it over all these years — something which is capable of floating her off her sandbank and towing her out of this sea of indifference,

20

idleness and uncaring boredom towards something more like life. The waiter has now taken his empty tray and gone back behind the counter to continue his conversation with his colleague and is looking at them again with that unseeing gaze — at both of them this time, as if she too, by some strange infection, had finally become incorporeal and invisible. It is of course quite possible that the waiter, after all these years of looking at people without seeing them from the other side of the counter, is not so wide of the mark after all with his conjectures. Though he would express it in much cruder terms, he may have in mind something quite similar to the subtler, more literary explanation which Elia might give him if he were prepared to listen. (The same explanation might also do for Ricardo.)

Elia prods gingerly at the tea-bag floating in the lukewarm water; the liquid colours slightly and turns cloudy in the stainless steel teapot, and a thin, faintly yellowish jet falls into the blue cup, while the invisible ape-poet indifferently drinks his coca-cola in a series of long, joyless swigs, having ordered it as he might have ordered anything else — you have to order something and he never drinks alcohol. He has no idea that Elia is annoyed by that lukewarm, watery, flavourless tea; that sort of irritation over trifles, those murderous impulses arising out of nothing at all, take years to become fully apparent. The poet puts down his glass and stares at Elia unblinkingly, with such a fixed, immobile, insistent and prolonged gaze that Elia herself begins to feel shy and almost embarrassed. Then he asks her whether she would be bored if he talked about himself. Not in the least, says Elia, assuring him — and realising that she means what she says — that, within certain limits and with certain rare exceptions, the one thing that never bores her is when people talk about themselves; they may be repetitive, platitudinous or pedantic, but they are never as boring as men pontificating

21

about politics, literature or matters of principle. When they talk about themselves, there is always the possibility, remote as it may seem, that something unexpected will come to light — some curious fact, some unusual or moving event, some genuine, unembroidered experience which stands out from the general run of melodramatic or farcical reminiscence because it possesses the spark of life.

As Elia said this, she laughed and pointed towards the glass of coca-cola; but Ricardo's face remained unsmiling and unblinking as before. And now he began to talk, and went on and on until Elia had finished her revolting tea and wanted to order some more, nasty as it was. What was worse, she had run out of cigarettes; she was waiting for a pause in the flow of words so that she could call the waiter, but the pause never came, because the words went on pouring out of the poet. He went on and on unendingly, with impeccable rigour and perfect order, without the slightest inconsistency, contradiction or unnecessary repetition. What he produced was a detailed, acute and even intelligent self-analysis. Perhaps, thought Elia, it had been carefully prepared and rehearsed, like that first discourse over the telephone. It contained everything: books that he had read, religious and mystical crises, his first homosexual experience mutual masturbation with another boy behind a desk piled with text-books and note-books, stained with ink and bearing the trace of the penknives of many generations of schoolboys, the two of them masturbating away together during the metrical composition class — but how funny, thought Elia, that it should happen precisely in the metrical composition class rather than during mathematics or geography; could it be that this too had been programmed in advance by the poet, with everything under control? — then there had been a short flirtation, a very short one, he emphasised, with Marxism. He went on to describe his achievement of mental and aesthetic

22

maturity, specifying that the aesthetic aspect was the more significant, though adding that in reality perhaps they were both the same thing. He now seemed to be approaching the end, and Elia reflected that the whole discourse was like a curious mixture between a pyschological essay and an introspective poem, like an elaborate, formal composition concerned more with symbolical values than with reality. It seemed to be based on a life without suffering or corruption. For although the poet and his school friend had been caught with their hands under the desk and their trousers undone (and that, in a school run by priests, must be something much worse than reading about springtime jungles in a seaside hotel), the episodes had the air of a rhetorical exercise, a beautiful literary passage about a squalid theme. The narrator seemed to be far above and far away from the events described. He was telling the story in the first person, but in this case the first person seemed to be no more than a literary device. Strange, thought Elia, how often the truth hides itself behind a cloud of sincere confessions, which are not nearly as transparent as they seem; could it be that Ricardo himself did not yet know it? What he was saying was very like a school oration, the speech of a conscientious pupil, first in his class, who mounts the rostrum on the last day of term to deliver a discourse which he has carefully learned, wearing his striped apron and blinking with his shortsighted eyes ... No, she thought, that's wrong — they don't wear aprons on these special occasions, and the boy will be wearing his glasses; but they've dressed him up in a Sunday suit, probably the one in which he went to his first communion. The suit is hot and uncomfortable, with long trousers, badly cut out of rough, harsh cloth, like the one Ricardo is wearing now. Ricardo *is* that schoolboy, she thinks; the ape wandering through the jungle on the track of the secret scent of a female on heat *is* a conscientious pupil

23

reciting a lesson which he has learnt by heart from beginning
to end, and reciting it very well.

But he had mercy on her in the end — there was something
moving about this clumsy but well-programmed lad — and
Elia had a chance to order some more tea; she also managed
to get a packet of cigarettes and a box of matches out of the
contemptuous waiter. For there can be no doubt that
Ricardo's classmates, with the possible exception of his
fellow-student in the metrical composition class, considered
him a bore and a swot; and ape-poets, swots and boys who
come top of the class do not smoke, although they sometimes
masturbate in the washrooms, or behind desks piled high
with books, with a special type of other boy — this point was
stressed as being particularly significant — stronger and
better looking than themselves, but much less intelligent,
and consequently easy to dominate. From her experience of
life, Elia found it hard to believe in this consequence, which
may have been a product of Ricardo's imagination. Anyway,
the well organised, precise calculations of the studious little
boy evidently do not extend to any idea of picking up the
packet of English cigarettes and offering one to his
companion, or of picking up the matches and offering her a
light. He probably cannot imagine that a nymph should want
to smoke.

Elia drinks her tea, which does not seem quite as nasty as it
did the first time, smokes her cigarettes, and listens to what
he has to say with serious understanding and real interest,
although she has to admit that she hasn't read Freud's
analysis of Leonardo. "What a pity!" says Ricardo, "it would
save us a lot of time if you had." He evidently finds fellow
students who have not done their homework something of a
bore. Elia is more at her ease now, and rather amused,
because the biographical summary is followed by a sort of
final balance-sheet covering the present position in the

24

professional, social, ideological and erotic-affective fields.
He again seems like a child — an egoistic, sickly child, a
child isolated in the corner of the playground, or hiding
under the table or in the wardrobe — as he describes his
qualities and his achievements, in his spoilt, eager, greedy
manner. There is something very moving (Elia suspects that
it may really be grotesque, but for some obscure reason she
finds it intimately moving) about this parade of logical
introspection carried almost to the point of becoming
ridiculous. Elia learned that the poet's professional pros-
pects are excellent, that his name is becoming known and
that his poems are having considerable success; she learns
that the poet, child though he is, is beginning to exercise a
certain amount of real power and authority. Ricardo's eyes
cloud over and he licks his lips as he speaks of real power
and authority.

But there is something missing in his life — and here for
the first time his speech loses its ordered structure and
suddenly becomes almost human. His voice takes on a tone
of warmth and reality and Elia becomes aware of his inward
wounds, itching, festering wounds, clotted with blood and
fetid with corruption. The narrator can no longer keep any
distance between himself and his story, or appease his pain
by converting it into art or literature. Elia realises that she
has been waiting for this moment of sorrow and truth from
the very beginning, waiting for the outbreak of the pain,
disquiet and doubt that are confusing Ricardo's imagery,
upsetting the structure of his discourse, and destroying his
farsighted plans and calculations. For now Ricardo is saying
something that he needed to say and had planned to say; but
he has lost the cheerful, flowery style appropriate to a
prize-winner's speech on the last day of term, which was also
the last day of a terrible, irrecoverable childhood. The river
of his speech has now broken its banks, and the air is flooded

25

with hoarse, clumsy, mutilated words which stream across the table to Elia and make her tremble.

There is something missing in his life, says the poet, something inexplicably missing, something hopelessly contrary to logic and justice. For the young ape-poet is not loved; and this fact seems to him monstrous and incomprehensible.

Elia feels a wicked temptation to tell him that he ought not to be so surprised or to think his case so exceptional, since the natural, almost universal rule in this world — a crazy rule, admittedly, for a sick world — is that no one feels himself sufficiently loved for long enough to matter; but she keeps calm and says nothing.

This mysterious and inexplicable fact, Ricardo continues, looking at her with the terrible, uncomprehending eyes of a lost dog, introduces imperfection and injustices into an otherwise admirable system. He is not loved; he never has been loved. For all his intelligence, brilliance and tenderness, for all the special capacity for loving that he feels in himself, for all his eager hunger for understanding and affection (which is common enough, thinks Elia, though she says nothing), other people do not seem to appreciate him, or even to notice him. The bespectacled schoolboy in his Sunday best has been pushed off the platform; they have taken away his sash, his purple and gold paper crown, his cardboard sceptre, his special diploma, and his three-coloured, three-flavoured ice-cream. And meanwhile all the other boys, who are not so kind, sensitive, intelligent and refined as he is, who lack the special capacity for loving he feels in himself — gross, brutal, mediocre lads who don't understand anything — have been given decorations and prizes, and run about the playground with their medals and their sweets and their girl-friends clinging to them, because a nightmarish mistake, an inconceivable miscalculation has been made, and the

26

scholastic exercises and examinations have been marked on the wrong principles. The poet, who has always been top of the class, top of all his classes, has been ignored and left alone in a corner to weep and lick his wounds. He sucks sticky mint caramels as he hides in the folds of the table-cloth, or cowers timorously in the moth-ball-scented refuge of the wardrobe, all alone and confronted by something which he, though always so quick, always the quickest of everybody, cannot understand and never will understand however often he tries, to the accompaniment of tears and caramels. There does not seem to be any love in the world for refined, intelligent, gawky boys, who dream of being dragged away by nymphs to the most tender and most unbridled of orgies. (There is no love in the world for anybody, thinks Elia from bitter experience, but she does not say so.) The result is that the nymphs never even look at him ... It is strange, amid all this cool drawing up of balance-sheets, this apparently brutal analysis, one thing remains unsaid, as if it were unknown to the poet or of no importance. He never says: "I have always been lacking in physical charm; I was an ugly child and I am an ugly young man."

Apart from not looking at him, the nymphs do not listen to him or show the least interest in what he has to say. (And what he has to say, thinks Elia, must be a single, obsessively repeated story; and it should be remembered that very few fifteen-year-old girls have read Freud on Leonardo.) Ricardo goes on to say that there is one girl who has listened to him and understood him, and has given him her friendship up to a point; this is Clara, who is intelligent enough to appreciate his intelligence, understanding enough to understand the fears and the loneliness of a timid boy, and sensitive enough to say the right thing or make the right gesture on almost every occasion.

27

But this must be a purely mental relationship, thinks Elia, with nothing physical about it; and it may turn out to be non-existent even on the mental side, since she has a feeling that Clara does not really like Ricardo, and since two people may have similar amounts of intelligence and sensibility and yet be unable to form a harmonious link because their intelligences and sensibilities are hopelessly different in kind. Clara's feeling for him must be something very like pity; or perhaps it is all a question of the almost insuperable difficulty that Clara finds in saying no, especially to someone who is both sensitive and unfortunate, and above all to someone who looks at her as Ricardo presumably does — with the look that is in his eyes now, as he speaks to Elia, having lost his usual mask of self-sufficiency and self-certainty for the moment. But however much Clara listens to him and understands him and supports him and learns things from him — even if she has read Freud on Leonardo at his request — Clara can never love him, says Ricardo, because she is in love with another woman. At this point Elia makes a sudden discovery, which however does not surprise her very deeply, because she is accustomed to sudden revelations of her own clumsy insensitivity and blindness, which prevent her from noticing things when they first happen. She realises that Clara is in love with her. Clara loves her with so desperate, exclusive, painful and total a love that she has no time for anyone else. Elia begins to think again, in the light of this new discovery, about the slim, big-eyed girl who has been following her and accompanying her everywhere for weeks past, if not for months past, doing her little favours and carrying messages, filling her room with flowers and sweets, and also with curious books which Elia would never have been tempted to buy, and is not now tempted to open — a girl who always seems to be there, in some corner of the house, but is so quiet, so passive, and so silent that you don't even

28

notice her presence. She is always ready to listen to what Elia has to say (Ricardo, too, gives her credit for being a good listener), always ready to shake her out of her moods of sadness, depression or discouragement, or to dry her hair or to make her a decent cup of tea. For Clara has learnt to make tea exquisitely well, warming the earthenware pot in advance, with a spoonful of tea for each cup and one for the pot and water that never quite boils — exquisitely made tea, nothing like this horrible tea-bag tea that you get in bars. She is also always ready to type a few letters for Elia, this helpful, silent and devoted girl; and Elia has sometimes wondered, though never with excessive interest, why Clara spends so many hours at her place, ever affectionate and ever ready to do anything to help, and has always concluded (right up to the present moment of revelation) that Clara must have very little to do now that she's finished or almost finished her university examinations, and that she must undoubtedly feel uncomfortable in her parents' house — Elia went there once to pick Clara up in her car and has memories of a grey façade in a narrow, squalid street. So Clara probably feels she has found a second and more comfortable home in Elia's place up on the sunny heights of the city. Elia, in fact, has made use of Clara without bothering her head about her or paying her much attention — she just found her there one day and didn't even ask herself where on earth the girl had come from. And now Elia has suddenly learnt — not from Clara, who has never allowed herself the faintest allusion to the matter or taken any steps in that direction at all, but from a third party — that Clara is in love with her. It is very strange (what an amazing girl she is! thinks Elia) that Clara, loving Elia as she does, has nevertheless encouraged her to make up stories about apes and virginal poets and jungles in springtime; it is very strange that she has been willing to serve as a messenger and perhaps even as an accomplice.

29

Or perhaps, thinks Elia, the whole thing can be explained as follows. Clara has a very flattering picture of Elia and a very unflattering idea of the poet; she can never have seen Ricardo as anything but a self-centred and unattractive boy. She puts up with him not because she admires his poetry (though she does), not because she thinks she can learn anything useful from him (she doesn't), but because she is extremely sympathetic and sensitive to the loneliness of others. Clara has no idea — and nor had Elia before today — that a woman may be overcome by a curious, ambiguous fascination at the thought of an obscure adventure, half sordid and half fantastic, with elements of the most miserable squalor and elements of high literature. Not knowing this, Clara could not foresee the possibility that this first meeting would lead Elia and Ricardo on to any further developments; she would assume that Elia could not possibly take seriously the pretensions of this clumsy, graceless, slightly ridiculous, utterly self-centred schoolboy. It's not as if he were a universal genius like Leonardo; he's just an unhappy, ill-treated little boy, licking his wounds and sucking his caramels under the table-cloth or in the depths of the camphor-scented wardrobe. That may be why Clara saw nothing wrong in encouraging Elia's fables about mating time in the jungle and about uninitiated young apes — creatures so very different from the well-dressed, blond-haired, elegant, mature men who seemed to be the official lovers of her friend — in a supreme effort, a desperate attempt to alleviate, at least for a few days, the omnipresent boredom, the lethal tedium and the destructive anxiety that afflicted Elia. That greedy, insatiable, all-devouring tedium might perhaps be relieved by fantasies based on an improbable story, thought Clara, which could naturally never be translated into reality, but which in fact did seem able to arouse Elia from her lethargy and amuse her, though Clara

30

could not understand why — and nor, for that matter, could Elia, wrapped up in herself as she was and blinded to the real world surrounding her.

There were more cups of tea-bag tea and more glasses of coca-cola in bar-room corners (nearly always the same bar, in point of fact), on various mornings and evenings, and even once on a Sunday morning, when Elia couldn't manage Sunday evening or any time on Saturday, and Ricardo couldn't wait till Monday to see her again. So it was Ricardo who suggested meeting on Sunday morning on this occasion, and he had to admit that Sunday mornings did not necessarily have a flavour of milky coffee and mothers with noisy, strawberry-guzzling children; because the café was still half empty, and in any case strawberries and cream (as Elia remarked with pretended dismay) were not among the things that it offered. Sitting there with Elia, he felt as if he had plunged into an icy river after her — first of all a shock which left him motionless, stiff and paralysed, and then the blood suddenly returning to his veins, like the crack of a whip, restoring life and mobility to his limbs. After this the world consisted only of the two of them in the middle of the river and everything else lay remote and inaccessible in the world beyond its banks. This applies even to the waiters, who have ceased to exist so far as Ricardo is concerned, though Elia uneasily points out that they are contemptuous and bored, busily engaged in investing the two of them with invisibility; from time to time they let her become partly visible again and then they stare at her with a faint smile of veiled reproach or frank sarcasm; but Ricardo cannot understand why any of this should matter to Elia, while they are clad in the armour of their love, protected by the ice of their river. Many intimate confessions and long-kept secrets

31

have passed between the two of them; Ricardo knew that he had found his ideal confidante, and smiled as he told her so; and Elia, too, had opened her heart to Ricardo, though her confidences seemed somewhat banal to the young man. She spoke hesitantly, looking into his eyes as if testing the ground to see how much further she could push ahead with her truth, with the heavy burden of her truth, without plunging her burden and herself into the depths of the marsh through which she was advancing. That laborious, fearful advance was inspired by the hope that if Elia and her truth won through to the far bank, Ricardo would play the part of a true confidant and reach out a hand, redeeming her for ever and freeing her from her private hell. But though Ricardo firmly believed that he had listened to her with genuine love, with deep and significant tenderness, and though he had punctuated her speech with intelligent and appropriate observations, the fact is that he felt deeply alarmed — all the more so because Elia too seemed to be frightened — and also felt a deep distaste during the few moments when she seemed about to emerge from the marsh with her burden of unavowable secrets, looking very like a lost child, a desperate little girl who looks round for support and may burst into tears at any moment. Ricardo stopped her at that point, on the very bank of the marsh, hoping that she would throw off her burden and let it sink, heavily and soundlessly, into the muddy waters behind her, after which she would finally emerge into the light of day as the nymph she used to be. The eyes of the nymph, which had nothing childlike about them, shone for a moment with a dark, angry flame — and then Elia laughed, squeezed his hand tenderly, and began talking about Rimbaud, or the drawings of Beardsley or the Jews of the Village. Ricardo gave a sigh of relief, realising that she had understood, and that she was grateful to him for preventing her from yielding to a moment of temptation and weakness. If she had said more, she might have besmirched or shattered something precious, destroying it for ever, since neither of them had any use for broken and mended china, or for clothes which still show faint, indelible stains after they have been cleaned. She might have destroyed the exquisite pair of images of themselves that they were planning and creating — images which reflect and multiply each other unendingly like a pair of facing mirrors, and which were admirably appropriate to the special circumstances. Those circumstances, Ricardo reflects, have been chosen and invented by himself, perhaps with some help from Elia. The two images are so appropriate, so exquisite, so brilliant, so deliciously literary, so intelligently unconventional, that it seems rather a waste that the only witnesses of their story should be a couple of waiters (and mocking, offensive waiters at that, according to Elia), a few readers of the sporting press in the mornings and some pairs of lovers billing and cooing in the evenings — people who either do not notice them at all, or give them a single, surprised glance and no more. And yet it's a beautiful story, thinks Ricardo, a story constructed with discriminating, loving, conscious care. He remembered a remark made by Elia one day, at the moment when she emerged nymph-like from the marsh and a look of disenchantment and anger passed across her eyes. She said that it was precisely the aesthetic side of the story, its implacable, orderly, programmed organisation, its painless, deodorised quality compared with the story he had told her at their first meeting, for example, and its remoteness from suffering, corruption and chaos, that prevented them from really loving each other. An inexplicable note of bitterness in her voice alarmed Riardo, because it seemed to contain a threat of a reproach, which however failed to reach its target. In spite of Elia's words, Ricardo considers that the story which he is inventing and creating is identical with the story

33

that she is inventing and wants to create. No other woman in the world — not even Clara, no, definitely not Clara — could adapt herself to the situation with so much precision and intelligence, or complete the picture with such a wealth of nuances and so sensitive a touch.

On one of the last occasions when they met in a bar, Ricardo suddenly showed signs of shame and even repentance, and angrily accused himself of having broken the rules of their game and betrayed their pact. They had come to a mutual agreement at their first meeting that they would not fall in love with each other, and now he realised that he did love her. This was supposed to be a startling and painful confession; but both of them had seen it coming and knew it to be inevitable. In spite of this, Ricardo's declaration had something frighteningly truthful and sincere about it. Elia at once adopted a discreet, understanding attitude, with a touch — only the slightest touch — of irony and a faint stirring of profound emotion: the right attitude for an exquisite woman who has just heard a young poet confess that he loves her, and loves her against his will; that he hasn't been able to avoid falling in love with her (and how flattering that must be for her, thinks Ricardo). Elia does not overreact to this announcement, nor does she pretend not to have heard it. She seems to accept it as a foreseeable and not too disastrous event, as she squeezes his sweaty hand, gives him an understanding smile and says "Don't be frightened — I am not going to hurt you." Sensitive, shy, unloved young poets nearly always fall in love with older women, exquisite, intelligent women — especially if they are very beautiful and listen to the poets' confidences in secret corners of half-empty bars. Elia smiled at this, squeezed his hand affectionately and delicately drank some of the tea that she said she found so revolting, and revived their eternal discussion of aesthetic matters — not Rimbaud this time, nor

34

Beardsley, nor the Jews of the Village, but the metaphysical poets. There is undoubtedly a feeling in the air, thinks Ricardo — it started with me but she's got it too — that we're acting out a sort of drawing-room charade. Both of us love subtlety, and this is a subtle and sophisticated game, the disinterested and therefore fruitless, but highly enjoyable performance of a minor masterpiece. Both of us, thinks Ricardo, realise that we have never previously made so many intelligent remarks in such a short space of time.

A few days later, Elia was alone at home. She had an appointment with Ricardo, one of their many appointments in the upholstered corners of more or less shady cafés, and the time for their meeting had arrived. She knew that the young ape-poet was waiting for her, and he must have already ordered his coca-cola some time ago, and that his impatience and terror at this first instance of her being late — for she has never kept him waiting before – must be becoming more and more unendurable with every minute that passes. The poet cannot bear to take risks, unless they are risks planned in advance by himself, and he is no good at dealing with the unforeseen — possibly, thinks Elia, because of the depth of his basic insecurity, because of the difficulty he has found in moving naturally and carrying out normal actions in a world which has been hostile to him, so that even now, when he has overcome many of his difficulties and left them behind, he still feels the need to keep to countless precise little rules and obessional habits, the need to retain various minute, indispensable certainties. He would rather pass a whole day without seeing Elia than suffer the intolerable uncertainty of waiting for a telephone call that might not come. From the beginning of their association, they have worked on the principle of using each meeting to establish an unalterable time and place for the next one, though the poet would in fact have preferred to set up a rigid timetable to be followed week by week for the rest of their lives. Elia has understood his feelings and fallen in with most of his suggestions. Never before has she let time pass by like this, let the minutes run on, although she is dressed ready to go out, and knows that he must already be waiting for her; although she can feel his anguish and terror in her own nerves. Then suddenly she seizes the telephone, though this is not what she planned; she hadn't planned anything and hadn't even realised — though she does now — that she had really delayed her departure in order to have a reason for making this telephone call. She dials the number with schoolgirl clumsiness, with adolescent haste, half afraid that she won't be able to say anything when she gets through, because for the moment her maturity has deserted her and she feels as eager, shy and anxious as if she were only seventeen. But her voice comes out normally, calm and musical as usual, gentle yet unhesitating as ever, asking him to come to her now, to come to her at once in her empty house. For a moment she is afraid that he won't dare to come; but there is nothing he won't dare to do now, this clumsy, awkward boy, because he is more afraid of losing her than of anything else. He arrives in the shortest possible time, silent and trembling but determined, and Elia greets him with a smile, more nymph-like than ever, takes his hand and leads him through the dark hall to the drawing-room, where they sit down on the sofa, their bodies sinking into the soft cushions. She pours out two glasses of sherry — no thought of coca-cola or tea this time — although the poet protests that he does not drink. Then they sit stiff and tense at opposite ends of the sofa, their recently acquired confidence and intimacy lost for the moment. She looks fixedly into his eyes, and he sustains her gaze. Then she slowly reaches out her hand to him, slowly and laboriously, as if he were

36

light-years away. The poet took her hand in his and suddenly seemed to understand. He realises, thinks Elia, that he has been given the magic key which opens the little cupboard with the sweets in it and the big cupboard where all the toys are kept — both the real toys and the imaginary ones which filled the games of his childhood and the dreams of his adolescence. What he feels during those first few moments is not exactly sexual desire. It is as if you had spent innumerable years staring through a shop window at the books, sweets and trains on the other side of the glass, and suddenly someone seized you by the scruff of the neck and the seat of the trousers and pulled or pushed you into the shop, saying: "Grab anything you like, it all belongs to you!" Or like suddenly finding yourself in Venice at the age of fourteen, which had happened to Ricardo. Elia could see him there now, as he had described himself to her, looking out of a hotel window over a canal, with his hands grasping the window-sill and his cheeks wet with tears. No, thinks Elia, what Ricardo is feeling now is not really desire; he is too surprised, alarmed and deeply stirred for that. It is more like a kind of intoxication or vertigo — he even looks physically giddy. It is a strange feeling, greedy and timid, incredulous and exultant; a feeling that drives him inevitably on towards an immediate, symbolical possession, visual or tactile, of the beloved object. He is like a little boy with nothing nice to eat who suddenly discovers, on a dish covered by a glass dome, the most wonderful display of sweets. He has no alternative but to pile them all up on his own plate and take them all away to his own table, although he doesn't even feel hungry and there is little chance that he will be able to eat them all. Real, physical possession will have to come later, thinks Elia with a smile: this will go on too long and lead to nothing for the present. Yet this was the right time for her to establish a hold on him, to make him her own, perhaps for ever. For Elia is

like a shop-window overflowing with wonders, like a magic
table covered with the most improbable dainties, like a
lovely city offering itself naked to the curious gaze of an
adolescent, like Venice seen through the eyes of a fourteen
year old boy, more beautiful than it could ever be for an
adult. The nape . . . the back . . . the breasts . . . with much
tugging he got her pullover off, and wrenched clumsily at the
catch on her brassiere; she laughed and waited and didn't
help him. Finally she was naked from the waist up. The boy
took possession rapidly and without any pleasure, anxious
only to establish his territorial rights, to plant flags on all the
islands and peaks just to prove that it all belonged to him.
Enjoyment can and must wait until a later stage. The tips of
his fingers run over every inch of warm, soft skin, every inch
of her shoulders, nape, back and armpits — there is a soft
down, like the down of a bird in the armpits. His fingers run
over her breasts — and what a surprise is provided by the
vibrant, erect nipples, like fleshy plants struggling upwards
towards his fingers and towards the light. Then he touches
her trembling ribs, and the smoothness of her stomach
down to her navel. He takes possession with his burning lips
which really do feel scorchingly hot on Elia's skin, and he
takes possession with his clumsy, rough, greedy hands. It's
all new to him, thinks Elia, all unexplored, unknown
territory. When Ricardo pulled down her jeans and pants,
Elia got impatient with this partial nakedness, this
conglomeration of clothing round her knees, and she whip-
ped them off and tossed them aside. Ricardo ran his lips, his
tongue and his fingers over her belly, her *mons veneris* and the
hollow between her thighs; and then, much to her surprise,
he begged and implored her to take off her sandals — a
strange request, she thought, after he had laid bare and
taken possession of the rest of her on his own initiative and
without any sort of previous consultation; apparently her

38

original gesture of gazing into his eyes and holding out her hand to him had been authority enough for that. Elia slowly took off her sandals and her socks, and the boy, screwing up his eyes, hugged her feet against his chest, brought them down to the level of his groin, and lifted them up again to cover them with kisses; he talked to them, sucked them, licked them, cooed over them and rocked them in his arms. Elia wasn't sure whether this was a scene from some novel, or merely from a film by Buñuel; it seemed unlikely that it came from the life or works of Leonardo. Anyway, the poet had now closed his eyes completely and lost his breath, sitting there with her feet again resting in his lap. That seems to be the end of his curious, desperate anatomical inventory: "The Various Parts of the Female Body." This inventory is not based on anything read in a book, nor on the words of a poet, nor on drawings, nor on photographs like the ones which he keeps hidden from the searching eyes of his mother at the bottom of a drawer in his cupboard, nor even on those films which stirred and alarmed him so deeply when he saw them at Perpignan. This is real flesh at last, living and fresh and scented, such as he had always desired and always dreamed of. For he must always have suffered from its absence, thinks Elia, always have felt a hopeless longing for the bright, living flesh of women, ever since the days when two little boys — one the cleverest in the class and the other the best looking — indulged in mutual masturbation during the metrical composition class, and hid pornographic books and pictures of naked women under desk lids or between the pages of textbooks. Elia imagines how they would watch and follow the girls as they came out of school. Her poet, she thinks, would never dare to pull a mane of golden hair or a black pigtail, or to lift a pleated blue skirt with a rude hand, though he would eagerly watch for the moment when one of his more daring companions would do so, giving him a brief vision of

39

thin or sturdy but generally shapeless thighs amid the swirling skirts, and a half-guessed-at glimpse of white embroidered pants or pink briefs. Sometimes other boys (of the sort who didn't waste time fiddling about in the metrical composition class but tackled the problem in a much more straight forward way in the lavatory) behaved in a still more daring manner with the girls, hitting them viciously, clumsily, hard enough to hurt — Elia can still remember the pain and the shame she felt when this happened to her — hitting them between the legs, on the buttocks and where their breasts were beginning to develop. The girls screamed, angry or excited — angry *and* excited, thinks Elia — and those cries redouble the excitement of the boys, and the girls learn the art of womanhood amid this strange mixture of insult and flattery, of resistance to aggression and provocation of further attacks, beginning to play a squalid game which they will have to go on playing for the rest of their lives, sometimes confusing it by a strange irony with the pursuit of love . . . Ah, the female body! How Ricardo had dreamt of its hidden mystery from childhood onwards, how he had pursued it endlessly down winding and dubious paths! It had always been present in his yearning heart, always clear and certain in its remote reality. Much less certain had been his hopes of ever catching up with it. And now the chase seemed to have reached its end.

This rare animal, thinks Elia, must seem to him to belong to a different species, perhaps inferior but undoubtedly different although it exercises a sort of perverse dominion over the sons of Adam. This unknown animal, about which the thoughts of Ricardo and the other boys have circled over since they were old enough to think, still seems mysterious, alien and dangerous to all of them, and especially to Ricardo, who has no sisters or cousins, not even any woman or girl neighbours who often visit his home, so that there is no female figure in his life, unless we count the pale and unapproachable image of his mother, who does not know the meaning of tenderness or affection, or his confused memories of countless little girls and older girls whom he has followed after school or during his more recent solitary wanderings, spying on their movements in the streets and squares of the city, or the ambiguous figure of Clara, who is so like Ricardo in her inexperience and her timidity, thinks Elia, that he probably does not regard her as a woman . . . And now this rare animal has voluntarily given itself up — voluntarily but at my instigation, thinks Ricardo — allowing itself to be cornered here on the sofa, trapped amid the down cushions, amid the dusty smell of the rows of books standing on the shelves and the muted street noises which come through the open window and lap softly about them. Pullover and brassiere have been put aside, pants and jeans, shoes and socks are scattered over the carpet. Elia's feet, the one part of her that he could not undress without asking for permission, lay naked, firm and soft in his lap. Long desired, secretly feared, the quarry was finally within the ape's grasp . . . though it might be nearer the mark to say that the ape-poet was approaching for the first time the bottomless trap into which he was destined to fall, the trap which must now inevitably swallow him up, and from which he cannot now turn back, in spite of all his anxieties and fears and nightmare visions. And it needed me, thought Elia, to produce this effect, this resolute determination not to turn back despite all his fears; it needed a woman who would seem sweet and gentle to his eyes, in spite of her casual manner and mocking smile, because that smile was balanced by a look in her eyes which she hadn't been able to hide this time and which he had certainly noticed. They are eyes which have known all the sorrows of the world, eyes capable of redeeming every kind of nostalgic longing. Elia also has very

41

soft, gentle, caressing hands, and she is sure that they evoke strange maternal images in Ricardo's mind, images which he has never known before, because no woman in the world could be less like Elia than his mother. Motherly, gentle and protective as she is, and expert in the arts of love, Elia knows that she looks quite different, as she sits by his side on the sofa and leans her head on his shoulder with her eyes shut, running a hand lightly through his hair. How lonely I am, thinks Elia, and how tired. She looks almost like a little girl nestling softly at his side. He doesn't mind this change of tone, in fact he likes it. It frees him from almost all his fear of Elia, and from every trace of the overwhelming terror he used to feel for women in general. And now it is as if Elia had a magical insight into his most secret fears, for when the anxious, timid boy reaches the point where he feels obliged to take off his trousers, she stops him with a gesture — without opening her eyes, as if she knew what was happening by intuition. "No, not yet, not today," she said. "When?" asked Ricardo, and Elia replied "On Monday." Ricardo uttered a sigh of relief, and Elia was sure that he felt happy and comforted, because the interval of three days which she had given him was exactly right, just what he needed to accept the offer and get used to the idea and overcome his last fears, to convince himself that he is the hunter and not the hare. Elia lies back along the sofa, with her head propped up at one end of it, and the boy kneels beside her, and lays his burning cheek against her smooth, delicate belly, against her soft thighs, soft and bright as those other thighs glimpsed long ago amidst the swirling of pleated skirts and embroidered linen, suddenly lifted up, with a clumsy, brutal gesture, by his more daring companions, whom he had envied for so many years. And now the ugly, diligent, conceited, timid poet has outdone all his school-mates, and has become their unquestioned leader.

42

Clara received a telephone call which she could not understand, though the voice at the other end of the line was clear enough. It was the same voice that had been punctually, precisely and remorselessly keeping her informed about developments every day, sometimes calling several times in the course of a single day. Clara didn't want to listen, but the voice ignored her dismayed protest, and went on keeping her posted about the progress of the story, as if it were an essential part of some perverse game for her to know about it. Ricardo would grab her, so to speak, and compel her to look through the keyhole, force her to watch what was happening inside the room; it was not enough for him to have her as an accomplice; she had to be a spectator as well. Or perhaps this was part of a complicated act of revenge . . . The voice would go on and on, despite her efforts not to listen, telling her about the words, the presents and the first kisses that had been exchanged by the pair of them, the other two, who were putting on their act inside the bedroom and leaving her outside the door, but insisting on her keeping her eye to the keyhole. Those exchanges had taken place in a series of more and more disreputable bars, where they were less and less likely to see anyone they knew; the meetings grew steadily longer, and the conversations steadily more intimate — more intimate and also more sincere as far as Elia is concerned, thinks Clara; Elia's words must be sincere, in view of something that the poet has admitted, with a shudder of distaste or fear, something which does not belong to the story that he acts out and relates with such relish, something which he mentioned inadvertantly, or perhaps to exorcise his fears by passing them on to Clara, as he has been doing for years. At certain terrible moments, he says, (though perhaps they are merely inconvenient and embarrassing moments), Elia seems to turn into a little girl, a lost child . . . he regards this image of her as a momentary aberration, since the picture of

43

a badly hurt little girl trying to win free of the marsh with her heavy load of dreams does not fit into his story, so that he has to restore her to her proper place without delay, and banish the inopportune image. They give each other more and more precious presents, Ricardo goes on; but then Clara reflects that this is probably only true of the presents that Elia gives him, for she knows that Ricardo is quite incapable of letting go of anything he really values, even now, when he is carefully playing the part of an ideal lover. Clara knows, from his own lips, that Elia has given him a book by Colette, beautifully illustrated with water-colours of flowers, gardens and cats, which she had often looked at with Clara in the past. Ricardo went on with a slow and remorseless description of Elia's body — the golden down on the back of her neck, her slim thighs, her pink nipples — while Clara heard every word he uttered, because she couldn't stop listening, much as she would have liked to. Then he gave her his most important news, repeating it three times in almost identical words, the magical, conclusive words which were apparently to close the first chapter of his story and seal his final victory. "On Monday I'm going to bed with Elia," he said, "Elia and I are going to bed together on Monday. Elia has promised that it'll be this Monday." But is that victory a victory over Elia, wonders Clara, or over his class-mates, or over me? Even after a further repetition of those triumphant words, Clara could not understand him; she said "That's fine!," and put the receiver down without even saying goodbye. She took it off again a moment later to stop him ringing again with more news, or, worse still, ringing again with the same impossible, unbelievable news, with a repetition of the same statement in varying tones of arrogance and euphoria. Clara sat silently huddled up in her armchair by the unhooked telephone, and made a terrible, painful attempt to understand. If only I could grasp what's happening between them, she thought, if

44

only I could understand this story, which makes me sick every time I think of it though I can't think about anything else, then I might be able to accept it, as I have accepted so much odd and eccentric behaviour from Elia in the past, so many arbitrary, capricious and even cruel actions. For Clara has learnt all about Elia's immense discontent, and enormous boredom; in hours and hours of loving, silent observation, and more hours of tirelessly, unceasingly thinking about her, Clara has sounded the unsuspected depths of Elia's loneliness, and knows or guesses the most secret hiding-places where Elia conceals her sorrowful disenchantment. Clara sees Elia as a lovely and wonderful being, far above everything and everyone who surrounds her, infinitely superior to everyone Clara has ever met; and yet she reluctantly has to admit to herself, although never, never to Ricardo, that there is something in what he says when he makes the provocative and wounding assertion that Elia is just another bored woman — very attractive, of course, and perhaps more intelligent than the others, but still caught in the same trap of tedium and dissatisfaction. Clara knows that Elia is often bored and impatient, because things never seem to turn out as they should, and she has frequently seen her give vent to these feelings at the expense of the rare and precious furniture that she buys in the antique shops, or of the pictures and sculptures and ceramics which her artist friends give her from time to time. She no longer likes these pieces of furniture and works of art, or at least no longer cares about them. (Her interest in them, thinks Clara, was intense but short-lived; it was like a compensation for something missing in her life, something of which Clara is aware only by the vaguest intuitions, and of which Elia herself probably has no very clear idea.) Elia ceases to care about those things as soon as they arrive in her house and are allocated a place in one or other of her rooms. It is a beautiful house, but has something provisional about it, a certain air of the transit camp. Elia often gives things away to the first person who praises them or asks for them. She has a reputation for being extremely generous, though Clara knows that in most cases she simply does not care about things, so that it costs her nothing to part with them. (But Elia did care about that book by Colette, which Ricardo must by now have dumped among the books piled on the floor of his bedroom, as if it were one of them.) In most cases, Elia is not so much generous as indifferent. Clara has seen her vent her discontent and boredom impartially among her servants and her friends, apparently lumping friends and servants together in a single mass, to which she pays little attention and in which she sees little difference. Elia had in fact confessed to Clara, with some surprise and embarrassment, that her lovers often complained that she sometimes treats them like servants; and Clara reflects that it is quite possible that she also sometimes addresses servants in the manner appropriate to friends or lovers. Elia sometimes finds all these people exhausting or irritating, though hardly ever to the point of wanting to sack her servants or break with her lovers. (Elia might express it differently thinks Clara with a smile, forgetting Ricardo and his terrible telephone calls for a moment; Elia might talk about sacking a lover and breaking it off with her maid.) She is never sufficiently irritated to set about introducing a little order into a household which in many ways resembles a mad-house, or to try to modify or limit her circle of acquaintance. And how unworthy of Elia that society is, thinks Clara; though what society could ever be anything else? Anyway, most of these people only exist for Elia as minor actors in her fantasies or as part of the audience. It is in this society that she watches the coming of age of her boredom and the flowering of her disenchantment. When her husband and her children are at home, they seem to be in

46

transit, like the furniture, the pictures and the ceramics — always on the point of taking off to New York on a business trip, to Chamonix on a ski-ing holiday, or to Cambridge to perfect their English. Some of the time, perhaps even most of the time, thinks Clara, Elia may honestly believe that she loves them, or might love them, or has always loved them; she may be glad when they come back home from their summer school or their ski-ing holiday, or their conference. She may go to fetch them, from some distant city or from the airport, and they may move back into their bedrooms and pick up their places at her table again. They may bring her presents and tell her what they have been doing and it may be perfectly true that Elia loves them; but it is also true that they have never brought fulfilment to her life — which Ricardo would undoubtedly describe as the idle life of a lazy woman or of a spoilt child; but Clara knows very well that this is not true, or at least that it is not the whole truth. Fulfilment is even further away now, when Elia's husband can only offer her an absent-minded tenderness, a lukewarm affection, in place of the splendid explosion of passion with which their marriage began, according to Elia herself.

There may have been a time, thinks Clara, during the first few months or the first few years of that marriage — and Elia's eyes grow dark and serious when she speaks of those early years — there may have been a time when her sorrows were dissipated and her pain banished to the most distant recesses of the dark forest. It was strange, thought Clara, that she and Ricardo, who disagreed in almost everything else about Elia, were both haunted by the same image of her as a lost, deserted little girl, though Ricardo tried to suppress that image, while Clara found it uniquely moving. Not that I can believe what Ricardo says about Elia, reflects Clara, he doesn't say what he thinks and talks mainly to hurt my feelings. Anyway, she sees Elia as a little girl while she thinks of her in those happier days, hoping to blossom out, to spread her wings, to escape from the marsh and throw off her nightmare load for ever . . .

And now the children are growing up so quickly, and soon won't need Elia at all; and there she is, so sensitive, so intelligent, and still so attractive, but so disorientated, so unoccupied, so doubtful about the possibility of beginning a career as a writer, a painter or a potter, as suggested by Clara. For Clara, in spite of Ricardo's sarcastic observations, still believes that she could do something worthwhile. But Elia is too tired or too insecure for anything like that; while on the other hand she is too ambitious and too demanding to settle for the hobby of running a boutique, an art gallery, an antique shop or even a bookshop. And so her boredom and discontent and impatience can find no other outlet but in the single, obsessive task — or vocation, or art, or vice — of love . . . locking herself up with a single plaything, to quote the mocking words of Ricardo. That was something Clara could understand; she had understood it very well, and had guessed as much from an early stage, before Elia had begun to confide in her about that sort of thing. She had guessed that two or three, or possibly more, of the friends who frequented the house and gathered round Elia at festivities had been or still were her lovers. And although Clara was of a jealous disposition, this development was too natural and inevitable, too banal and too unimportant to Elia herself, to arouse Clara's resentment. It was a mere pretext for Elia to escape for a few hours from the emptiness which was devouring her, just as the pictures and the antique furniture were a pretext. It was a way of escaping for a time from the marsh whose bottomless depths would probably swallow her up in the end. (And *that* will happen, thinks Clara with a shudder, when the heavy load of the past, the burden of dreams, begins to outweigh the insubstantial pageant with which she surrounds herself at present. Then the lost child will fall back into the mire, grabbing desperately for the last time at the plants growing on its edge, and will sink to the bottom, finally conquered by her dreams.)

For Clara has seen Elia sitting for hours and hours, sometimes for whole days, without getting dressed or doing her hair, sitting in front of the open window, listening to the children shouting in the courtyard below, or the song of the birds, of Clara's voice gently mocking or beseeching, or telling her stories. Sometimes Elia sits there stroking the cat as it dozes on her lap; sometimes she loses touch with reality so thoroughly that she doesn't even know whether her hand is mechanically caressing the fur of the cat or the similar agreeable softness of Clara's hair. At other times Clara has found her huddled naked at one end of the huge bed, with her face to the wall, and a bottle of sleeping pills on the bedside table, with no idea how many she has taken; and Elia has refused to answer any questions, refused to drink a glass of milk or a cup of tea, refused to try to get up from the bed or even to roll over so that Clara can see her face, silently chewing over her disenchantment and resentment like a lethal drug, many times more poisonous than the large, but never dangerous, doses of sleeping pills or sedatives that she takes. At other times Clara has seen her spend whole evenings in front of the television, seated or sprawled on the carpet, with her shoulders supported by cushions or leaning against the sofa, paying so little attention to the screen that she doesn't even notice if the sound cuts out or if the image is distorted; she continues to sit there with her eyes fixed on a screen where there is nothing to see but moving horizontal beams of light, or a snowstorm, or faces reduced to a grotesque parody by the loss of sound. This goes on until something happens to break the spell — some trifling external event, apparently of no importance, sometimes so insignificant that Clara cannot even identify it. Clara's anxiety, apprehension and fears are increased by her inability to find out what causes the trouble and what so miraculously cures it; she reflects that the mysterious cure might fail to materalise one of these days. But so far something has always done the trick — an unimportant external event, or some imperceptible change in Elia's mental state, a sudden change which makes her decide to break out of the circle of suffering and boredom; or perhaps it may be the presence of Clara herelf, with her desperate, affectionate insistence on staying with Elia and trying to help, with her timid caresses, as light and gentle as those of the cat. Perhaps Elia reacts to all this, thinks Clara, like someone waking up from a nightmare; possibly the same nightmare that is already shared by Ricardo and Clara, and which may well find a third home with Elia — the nightmare of a lost child struggling uselessly against the weight of the burdens on her back as she tries to get out of the marsh. Anyway something makes her wake up and undergo a sudden and total change of mood so that she leaves her bed, or the chair by the open window, or the cushions on the rug in front of the television. When that happened, Clara would wash Elia's hair with a creamy, sandalwood-scented shampoo, and dry it carefully, holding the hair-dryer in one hand and a silver hairbrush in the other, while Elia hummed a tune and laughed, or chattered like a sparrow. Then Clara would get quantities of clothes out of the wardrobe, so that Elia could choose a dress to match the golden colours of the morning, the rosy tones of the evening twilight, or her own changing moods; and sometimes — on one or two marvellous occasions — they had gone out together, just the two of them, to drink an aperitif and eat shellfish by the sea at Sitges. How gay and tender Elia was at those times, with her auburn hair billowing in the breeze! Or sometimes they would go to an Italian restaurant which both of them liked. Clara liked everything which pleased or amused Elia, and it was really Elia who decided that both of them liked the restaurant, or even that it was a special favourite of Clara's. Neither of them would ever go there with anyone else. Sometimes the two of them would go out together and meet various men friends and acquaintances; friends and acquaintances of Elia's, that is to say, for Clara does not like them at all, and suspects that Elia, too, often finds them terribly stupid, pedantic and boring. They talk in a sort of banal jargon which highlights the least attractive features of their class. This seems even nastier and more embarrassing in a man than in a woman. It is strange that Elia, alone in this society, does not talk in this way. Clara dislikes their commonplace remarks, their certainty that they are always right and their conceit; also the ostentatious way in which they flatter Clara, corner her, caress her, kiss her, fuss over her and compete for her attention. Sometimes they seem to want to protect her, as if she were a mysterious little creature from outer space, or one invented by the strange and lofty imagination of Elia. They seem to think she is the epitome of all that is new and modern, and also that she is terribly delicate and threatened with extinction. These are friends whom Clara would like to hate, because she is repelled by contact with them and by their voices and by the way they look at her and embarrassed by their admiration and their jokes; but she can't quite manage to hate them altogether because she knows that there are days — just a few — when they amuse and comfort Elia, and even help her in some strange way to stay alive. And Clara likes to see Elia manoeuvring among her friends, moving with such relaxed grace amid the throng, with her long legs, her boyish walk and her mane of auburn hair. (Ricardo says that Elia set out

51

with a vocation to be a red-head, but got weary and left off in the middle, as she does with everything.) She loves to see Elia's impertinent freckles and listen to her clear laugh, knowing that she is always ready to treat servants as if they were friends, or lovers as if they were servants. For Elia looks at her from time to time, in the middle of a remark addressed to someone else, and gives her an almost invisible wink; and then Clara thinks that the whole game is for her benefit, the whole comedy is in her honour and that what Elia says is really addressed to her, for her to hear so that the two of them can mockingly amuse themselves at the expense of friends and lovers. She likes to see Elia mixing with all these people, knowing that Elia is always the smartest, tenderest and prettiest person there. She likes to see her sparkle and relax and escape to some extent from herself, from the mortal sickness and the sombre thoughts that so often seize her and confine her to her bed, or the chair by the open window, or the rug in front of the television. Any incident which rescues Elia for a few moments from her depressing and heart-breaking fantasies, any stimulus which leads her to wash her hair, get dressed and go out of doors, seem acceptable and justifiable to Clara, whether the two of them go out to the beach at Sitges, or out for dinner in the Italian restaurant ("*our* restaurant", says Elia with a smile, passing her hand fleetingly through Clara's hair); whether it leads them into the shadowy auditoria of cinemas or theatres or concert-halls, or into crowded gatherings (anything over two is a crowd in Clara's eyes). These gatherings generally comprise a number of friends of the type just described, and also the ambiguous figures of two or three possible lovers — correct, elegant, well dressed, tall and nearly always fair-haired, almost always smelling of pipe tobacco or of lavender. These lovers are never nearly good enough for Elia, according to Clara, and this is one point on which Ricardo does agree with her. None of them are remotely capable of understanding Elia or helping her; but they are justified, in their own eyes and in those of Clara, if they can manage to amuse her for a few moments, or satisfy her feminine vanity; although men like that are not really in a position to flatter her, in her feminine vanity or any other vanity she may have. It's all right if they can make her smile or sing, or perhaps even give her what everybody calls pleasure, although Clara is not too sure what it is. She has always run her life in terms of love or failure to love, so that, for her, pleasure or the lack of pleasure are measured solely by the distance that separates her from the person she loves. She finds it difficult to imagine how those gentlemen, with their neatly clipped hair, their neatly clipped speech, their impeccably cut clothes, their polo sweaters or their pink shirts and Italian ties can give pleasure to Elia, who obviously does not love them, and seems hardly capable of picking them out from the shapeless mass of friends that surrounds her, or even of telling one lover from another. (Clara also finds it difficult to tell them apart.) How *can* they give Elia anything like what Clara imagines true pleasure to be? But Clara admits that it must be so, like many other things in Elia's life in which Clara can't share because she can't conceive of them as part of her own, but which she believes are really useful to Elia in some mysterious and inexplicable way.

And Clara did accept everything, she did try to understand everything, with a certain amount of success, right up to the beginning of this business with Ricardo, this stupid adventure which she had seen beginning to develop before her own unbelieving eyes. No, it was worse than that — she had been too blind to see what was happening. Clara realised that she had encouraged the affair at certain stages by allowing herself to be forced into a degree of unwilling and sometimes unconscious complicity. She had listened to Ricardo's

53

confidences — those excited, lyrical and delirious confidences, which were at the same time so planned and calculated, so fundamentally selfish. For Clara had been sorry for Ricardo for a long time, since before the year when they both entered the University. She had felt sorry for this clumsy, solitary, unloved boy, and she got into the habit of listening to him, even when the words of the lyric poet repelled her by their egoism, cynicism and pettiness. Her complicity began when she agreed not only to listen to him, but to repeat his words to Elia. But how had he managed to persuade Clara to do that? What endless syllogisms had he developed during what interminable evenings? Clara had seen the story as a piece of fantastic gossip which would be sure to amuse Elia, who was so fond of gossip and so fond of being amused. But this was right at the beginning, before any thought had crossed Clara's mind that Elia might feel in the least flattered or disturbed, or in any way involved. How could a woman like Elia be stirred by anything so clumsy, so literary in the worst sense of the word, so literary and so false, so basically greedy? These were the grubby longings of an unloved schoolboy, a graceless oaf, with greasy hair, pimply cheeks, squinting through his glasses, wearing wrinkled clothes a size too large for him. A boy who used to follow girls in the street with throbbing heart and dry lips, but never dared to speak to them, waiting for another man to come up to them, speak to them and perhaps kiss them on the eyes or the mouth. Ricardo never dared to approach prostitutes, either; they inspired him with an unconquerable, atavistic terror, which may have owed something to the prophetic warnings of his mother, which were always vague and ambiguous, and all the more frightening for that. After the death of his father, his mother probably felt it her duty to replace him in this advisory role, but she couldn't go beyond the vaguest and most indefinite of warnings, whether from

54

shame or from ignorance of the subject. Apart from his mother's words, Ricardo was also frightened by the hard, mocking eyes and disdainful lips of those women, so much more ready to show scorn than tenderness, and by their ugly, stereotyped gestures, when he watched them (as he sometimes did) of an evening in narrow, evil-smelling city streets, waiting to see other men accost them. (For years on end, Ricardo's pleasure had seemed to consist in spying on other people, in observing them from afar, and telling Clara all about it, although she found the subject uninteresting and indeed repellent, and only listened out of goodness of heart.) He would watch other men come up to those women and accost them and follow them up along, dark stair-cases, because he was afraid of prostitutes, just as he was afraid of the girls in his class, or shop-girls and waitresses in bars, whom he also sometimes secretly followed in the streets. Clara was sure of one thing, and indeed Ricardo himself had confirmed it several times — he used to imagine those girls adopting the positions and carrying out the actions which he knew from his researches into literature, drawings, photographs and films and of the kind he had seen in Perpignan, or taking part in other scenes of his own invention. And so Ricardo would masturbate, sighing and sobbing, and always afraid that his mother might burst into his bedroom at the most inopportune moment, with his mind full of pictures of girls seen in the street, in bars, or in the class-room, acting out unlikely scenes in improbable attitudes, until he abandoned all these games and began to occupy himself exclusively with the image and name of Elia, lying on his bed with wet cheeks, sweaty body and his lips pressed against the pillow. When Elia heard about this from Clara, she laughed and passed it over lightly, with a mocking gesture; but she didn't look at all disgusted and indeed seemed to be slightly flattered.

55

For months and years past, Ricardo had also been in the habit of staring at Clara, eyeing her legs and breasts and arms, in a way which used to make her feel terribly uncomfortable, and still does. It is worse even than the way Elia's friends sometimes stare at Clara and touch her, for there is nothing furtive or secretive about that. Everything about Ricardo has always been furtive and clumsy, and Clara had never been quite sure when her tolerance would give place to a feeling of overwhelming repugnance towards this immature, graceless boy. There had been one or two terrible occasions when he had put his trembling, insecure, moist, cold hand on her bare arm, her warm neck or her delicate knee, without even noticing that the contact made her sweat with anguish and fall into a chill, rigid, deathly trance.

A period of some days followed, during which Clara went to and fro with messages. She duly repeated Ricardo's words and the words of Elia. These were words spoken for her to repeat, spoken to involve her as an intermediary in their astonishing and fantastic game, which she sometimes thought might be dangerous for Ricardo (she couldn't imagine it ever being dangerous for Elia). Ricardo would inevitably be hurt when something happened which Clara regarded as inevitable and expected to happen soon. Elia, she thought, would do what she always did, and get tired of the game right at the beginning; she would break it off before the match had really begun. Clara felt somewhat guilty about the boy — about letting him fall into this trap, about using him in this way to give a few days relief to Elia's boredom and her usual springtime depression. It seemed wrong to let him form hopes which were bound to be disappointed. And yet he was so self-centred, so banal and so fatuous — how, she wondered, could he dare to aspire to the love of a woman like Elia? — that Clara soon dismissed these twinges of conscience. She reflected that, when the fatal moment came, she would be there, as ever, to support him, to listen to him, and to soften the blow. In any case, Clara had now lost control of the situation — if she had ever had any — and this had taken place quite a long time ago, before she could realise what had happened. Elia and Ricardo would continue their game without her; as an intermediary she was useful but not indispensable. Clara would have to let the story work itself out. At the end of it all there would be a period of weeks or even months during which she would have to listen to the hysterical lamentations of Ricardo, who would be more deeply wounded than ever. Clara would have to put up with his weeping like a child with a broken toy, with that look in his eyes like a dog that's been beaten and does not understand why, and with his interminable attempts to explain, by means of lengthy rational analysis, the reasons for something which is completely self-explanatory and obvious: the plain fact that Elia had played a silly game with him for a short time, and then dropped him before it could turn into a real, serious adventure.

Clara's mind goes back to Ricardo's last telephone call. She knows that Ricardo would not deliberately lie to her on such an occasion or about such a subject, but she also knows that what he said cannot be true; that his statement, repeated three times, in almost exactly the same words, must somehow be based on a misunderstanding or a mistake. She can't bear to imagine it. She is overcome by intolerable nausea, by a feeling of physical sickness that leaves her giddy, trembling and paralysed at the very thought of his soft, sweaty body, his panting, slobbering, impatient mouth, and his rough, clumsy hands touching Elia's delicate, smooth, sandalwood-scented skin (the milky, lightly freckled skin of a woman who set out with a vocation to be a redhead); or caressing her exquisite body, supple as the body of a child or a young girl, the auburn hair which flowed so smoothly down to her shoulders, her little, pale pink nipples and her long, shapely thighs. There *must* be some mistake, thinks Clara again and again, obstinately fighting her depression. Perhaps Elia expressed herself badly; perhaps she was joking; though that would not be like her. Perhaps Ricardo's crazy hopes and desires had made him think he heard something which had not been said at all. If the worst came to the worst, something would surely crop up during the next three days — even at the last moment, something must happen to prevent the unimaginable horror of those two ill-matched bodies meeting in intimate contact.

Elia spent the whole weekend indoors, hardly stirring from her bed during the three days that separated Friday's performance on the sofa (a broadly conceived scene for two which both had enjoyed) from the next little drama, which she had capriciously, voluptuously, perversely postponed until Monday morning. She had done so partly in order to still the last fears which she could see were still troubling Ricardo by artificially making things a little, just a very little, more difficult for him at the last moment; although in another sense she was making things easier for him by showing herself less impatient, less anxious, greedy and aggressive, and more serene and protective. The main object of the postponement, however, was to enable her to savour and prolong — for her own pleasure, for her own torment — that delightful yet intolerable excitement, that intensity of the imagination and the senses, which were probably Elia's only means of escape, the only form of intoxication of which she had always been capable. Elia knows that money and prestige cannot move her, and that the privileges of class mean almost nothing to her, probably because she has had them since she was very young and because, like many other

58

things, they give her a slight feeling of bad conscience. Conscientious twinges of this kind are however so remote and ineffective that they cause little discomfort, and do not cut our pleasures short or keep us awake at night. Elia reflects that she is bored by the exercise of power at the levels of which she has experience. Bored, that is to say, with the few forms of power that have lain within her grasp, though she has often made use of them, with varying results. Another thing she can't take seriously or regard as important is her own appearance, what other people call her beauty. She is too indifferent to be vain; and in any case the leggy, red-headed good looks, with their evocations of childhood and adolescence, do not really coincide with her own imaginary picture of herself, so that she often has a shock when she unexpectedly comes up against a mirror. Elia is sometimes alarmed when she realises how vast a number of aspects of reality are outside her circle of interests, and how few things have the power to touch her. For some reason that she does not understand — perhaps lack of ability or of staying power, perhaps because she has never been able to concentrate on one thing — she has left behind her a dark trail of unfinished tasks. This is especially obvious and especially painful now, when Clara keeps finding things in cupboards and book-cases — paintings and water-colours which Elia had almost forgotten, first chapters of novels, dramas or short stories, fragments of poems and even a guitar which Elia had used at one time to accompany herself when she sang. In this Clara sees proof of a talent that some day must inevitably find expression; but Elia knows that it is merely evidence of her lack of ability, which may be due to the fact that they told her when she was very young that her future would be one of marriage and general culture and that she would never have the courage, determination or enthusiasm which enabled a very small minority of women to break out of that circle.

59

General culture turned out to consist of great heaps of books which she devoured with undiscriminating diligence, plans for writing which came to nothing, repeated sightseeing visits to various cities, concerts, museums and art exhibitions. Marriage turned out to be a well paid occupation which took up little of Elia's attention and even less of her time, since it was obvious that her husband was fond of her and equally obvious that there was practically nothing for which he needed her, while Elia couldn't or wouldn't make her two children the central purpose of her life. How can you make your children the central purpose of your life, knowing perfectly well they'll soon grow up and leave you, and also knowing that their life is for them to live, and not to be scooped up and appropriated in its early stages by a parent as melancholy and dissatisfied, as capricious and ineffective, as yourself? You may be a bad mother, but you don't want to commit the ultimate crime of usurping, absorbing, vampirising the very existence of two other human beings. Elia has never had the faith and the driving force to make her a militant supporter of any cause. From a very early age, she has had no strong religious beliefs. She is too clear-sighted to be able to engage in philanthropy or any form of good works without dying of shame. She is too cowardly or lazy — or perhaps just too apathetic — to make a serious attempt to change anything. She can't even change the rhythm of her own life, the absurd arrangement of the furniture in her house, or the plans for the children's summer holidays.

Against this background, the intensity of her imagination and her senses to which we have already referred, and which had little enough to do with sex, was indeed the only escape, the only intoxication of which Elia had ever been capable since her childhood, or of which she ever would be capable until her death.

"Elia has no *small* vices," say her friends jokingly; and though Elia is not amused by this, it is true that she smokes very little, drinks very little, and has no interest in the experiences that can be derived from LSD or cocaine. Nor is she much interested in the experiences that can be derived directly from sex. There is nothing that can give her help, relief or comfort against the melancholy fact that she seems doomed to lead a life without purpose, which will end only in a disaster that she cannot understand but knows she cannot avoid. Her friends and lovers sometimes tease her by quoting "man has but a short time to live, and is full of misery." Elia does not reply, but silently thinks "then man should reach for the stars." Her only resource is that same intensity of the imagination and the senses, like a uniquely effective drug; but every day it becomes a little more difficult for her to obtain that relief. Gradually, inevitably, she has to increase the dose to achieve the same result. One might think (and it is in fact the truth) that Elia's life contains no possibility of pleasure or survival — no possibility of the minimum of pleasure necessary to ensure survival — apart from this single, irreplaceable drug. It is as if Elia's life consisted of just two elements: on the one hand, a series of brief attempts to give up or change the drug, which always come to grief because of her chronic inability to carry out her intentions; on the other hand, longer periods when she faces the impossibility of learning to live without the drug and devotes herself to the struggle to obtain further supplies, at any cost. Elia is often sick at heart to see how her past and future life are dominated by a spirit of sickly, inner expectation, by an unhealthy, insatiable thirst for that special intoxication which is her sole resource — an intoxication which has no direct link with sex, and which must not be confused with love, though Elia herself tried for years to do just that. (It cannot at least be confused with Elia's idea of what love

61

should be, or with any other form of love that had anything real, lasting or positive about it.)

And that terrible thirst would accept no substitutes. Elia's desires and needs were always fairly specific; but this thirst is so terrifyingly specific that it can only be satisfied by one single kind of liquor — something really splendid and delicious, or perhaps something uniquely repugnant . . . who knows? there have been years and years of dusty, lifeless drought, years and years of lethargy and of half animate existence, waiting for the rain which always comes unexpectedly however much you look out for it. The rain which can carpet the ground with an abundance of life, like a splendid firework display shining out in the darkest hour of the night, bringing with it an intoxication that has the same fantastic beauty as the monstrous, unscented flower that the desert cactus brings forth ten or a dozen times during its long and secret life. The pendulum swings regularly between utter drought and mad intoxication . . .

Although Clara lovingly watches Elia second by second, hour after hour, there are some things she has never been able to grasp, perhaps because Elia herself does not understand them. What is it that Elia wants and needs and seeks? What is the reason for that unappeasable anxiety, that devouring boredom? And where, Clara wonders, can a cure be found for that anxiety and that boredom? — for Clara does not realise that there is no possibility of change or development in Elia's character. Clara has heard Ricardo say this, but she does not accept it, and does not accept that Elia is incapable of overcoming any difficulty, because she is not and never will be a fully grown-up woman in one sense of the word. Elia is troubled at times by a faint but secretly painful doubt regarding her own position as a woman. She can never make out what other people mean by the phrase "a real woman", though she always feels it as a threat to her self, a

62

hidden danger, not unconnected with the disagreeable feeling that afflicts her when she unexpectedly sees herself in a mirror. Perhaps she can't be a proper adult for the same reasons that prevented her from ever being a proper child (though this is something that neither Clara nor Ricardo can possibly know about). She was always so different from the other children at school, in town or by the seaside, with her eccentric, benevolent parents, as benevolent and as inaccessible as gods; with her unrestricted choice of books and their dubious passages about rutting apes in the springtime; and with her long, solitary excursions, alone or with an unsuitable companion ... Eternal child or eternal adolescent, precariously making her way along a slack-rope swinging perilously above the terrifying void, with ambivalence in every movement, in search of the unlikely event which would implant that fatal thirst, the need for that fatal intoxication, in her heart for ever, without any possibilty of subsequent disentanglement!

And so Elia hardly stirs from her bedroom for the whole of that weekend. The school holidays have begun, and the passage of time is no longer marked by the cries of children coming out to play; but the birds continue to sing, most loudly at dawn and sunset, which Elia imagines must be the most favourable times for their love affairs. She lies naked on finely-woven, freshly ironed sheets, with that extra smoothness that comes from use. From time to time Elia rolls luxuriously over on to a cooler part of the bed, or turns her pillow to enjoy the fresh coolness of the other side for a moment, before it gradually begins to warm up. Elia tries to push away the cat, which keeps on snuggling up to her side, so besotted with feline affection that not even the unpleasant, sticky heat of early summer can persuade it to move off to the floor or the window sill. For three days Elia has hardly answered the telephone, hardly eaten anything, and hasn't even wanted to see Clara. Lying in the shadows, she has passed the time in feverish anticipation of the ebb and flow of her only intoxication, deriving both pain and pleasure from the delay which she has deliberately chosen, not to say programmed, though at times it is more than she can bear. Minute by minute, she has to overcome an ever-present temptation — a temptation which probably adds the final touch of exquisite perversity to her pleasure. She is tempted to ring Ricardo and tell him that there's no point in waiting till Monday and that she wants to see him at once. She is certain that Ricardo is spending the weekend in the same way as herself, shut up in his bedroom, feeling the same impatience and yet enjoying the same pleasure in delay. Elia knows, too, that it will disappoint him and spoil their story if she gives in now and calls him to her. She falls into a strange reverie, punctuated by fleeting visions of Ricardo's body — a skinny, smooth, almost hairless body, weak, clumsy and entirely at Elia's mercy — a body prepared for her by years and years of vague expectation, of concealed longing, of causeless anxiety. It has also been prepared for her by days and days of very definite desire; it is being gradually awakened to reality by the touch of Elia's own body, won back to physical reality from the shadowy world of dreams. Mental images like these are new to Elia; her previous love affairs have been more light-hearted, her previous passions less physical. She has never had thoughts like these about the irreproachable bodies of her tall, fair-haired lovers, with their impeccable technique and their smell of eau-de-cologne and expensive tobacco. The new images give an edge to her longing, an intensity to her anticipation of the pleasure to come, which she has never felt before. The sensation is delightful, but at the same time faintly alarming. It could mark the beginning of a new and dangerous stage in the irresistible onward march of her addiction. After the end of this affair, she might find that her craving would take a more specific and perhaps a more oppressive turn.

Early on Monday morning, Elia rang Clara and asked her to come and see her. Clara came at once, as she always did. During the short taxi ride to Elia's house, Clara was thinking that this urgent call was definite proof that Ricardo had made a mistake, that Elia was not going to sleep with him. Otherwise why would she have summoned Clara on this very Monday morning? Clara's face was very pale when she arrived; but Elia was too wrapped up in her own nervous impatience and disquiet to want to take any notice of that. Despite Elia's efforts, the thought worms its way into her mind that she and Ricardo are not the only two people who have just spent the weekend shut up in their bedrooms, scarcely stirring from their beds, and in great distress. Clara has been in the same position — and in her case the distress was absolute, unmingled with any element of pleasure or expectation, and relieved only momentarily by the hope that perhaps, after all, nothing would happen. Elia tried hard not to remember what Ricardo had said about Clara's love for her. Elia is quite incapable of attaching the same importance to the feelings of other people that she does to her own, and is aware of this fact. The thought of Clara's feelings gives her only momentary discomfort, because she reflects that she can easily put things right by taking Clara out to dinner or to the cinema, or by asking her to brush her hair. Only one thing is real for Elia at this moment, every other possible reality having been wiped out by the overwhelming fact that the time fixed for her meeting with Ricardo has now arrived and that he must already be waiting for her. It isn't exactly that she is ready to sacrifice everything and everybody to the intensity of her caprice — caprice is in any case the wrong word for an addiction to an intoxicant the lack of which drags us back into the deepest part of the marsh. In any case, if it were a caprice, it would still be a matter of life and death for Elia. In fact, however, it is something much more simple and more terrible: everybody else has ceased to exist for Elia, and she would be quite capable of walking bare-foot over their bodies without noticing that they are there, if she could see Ricardo — the one remaining reality in her life — waiting for her at the other end of the path. And so it is only for a few moments that Elia feels slightly uncomfortable while she explains the situation to Clara, who has gone very pale and is trembling a little. The situation is that Elia didn't ring Clara up because she wanted her to stay with her, or to go shopping together or to visit some gallery or to go out for a drink by the beach; she just wants Clara to stay in and wait by the telephone in case Elia's children ring her up from London or Cambridge, because Elia is going to be out for the whole morning.

Elia could see him waiting for her when she was still some way from the corner where they had agreed to meet — a skinny, clumsy young figure clad in a raincoat which had completely lost its shape, and can never have been much good anyway; it was also alarmingly long for him. And she wondered why her ape-poet had got himself up like that on this bright morning of early summer, without a single cloud in the blue sky. She finally concluded that Ricardo probably regarded the raincoat as part of the exotic disguise appropriate to a clandestine lover . . . Be that as it may, he is certainly in a bad state of nerves. Tormented by terror and desire simultaneously in the highest possible degree, he stumbled his way into the car, getting his raincoat caught as he did so, and couldn't manage to shut the door. Elia leaned smilingly across from the driving seat and did it for him. Then she rumpled his hair lightly with her hand, which

66

increased his comic resemblance to a disoriented ape; he was too sunk in reverie to think of smoothing his hair down again. Elia went on to give him a little welcoming kiss on the cheek, to which he did not respond. Nor did Ricardo manage to say anything to the boy who came out to meet them when Elia had parked the car in a small individual garage; he followed Elia and the boy through a labyrinth of long, tortuous corridors, full of curves and changes of direction. At each turning the boy paused and put his head round the corner before they went on, to avoid the risk of any unfortunate encounter. Ricardo followed Elia and the boy into a lift which looked as if it had been borrowed from some luxurious bathing establishment of the end of the nineteenth century. Finally, he followed them into an incredible bedroom . . . The programme-besotted, know-all poet was in a new situation where he knew nothing; and his embarrassed silence delighted Elia. She enjoyed seeing him finally confronted with something that he couldn't have planned in detail in advance, even on a theoretical basis . . . It'll only be like this the first time, thought Elia, on subsequent occasions he'll recover the nervous aplomb and the shaky obstinacy which allow him to speak his mind and even impose his will. But on this occasion Elia had to do the talking to the boy herself, after he had unsuccessfully asked Ricardo three times which room they wanted. She asked for the one which she knew to be the craziest and most bizarre of all. Strange, she thought, that you can still find this sort of thing, this fantastic type of room in the houses of assignation in a city where everything is being changed so rapidly. She was sure that this would be in keeping with the poet's intimate desires, with his deepest dreams; he was a persistent reader of pornographic novels, deeply possessed by the desire to fuse sex and literature together; and no bedroom could be more literary than this one, with its bogus decoration, all flesh-tints and papiermâché, reminiscent of the most fantastic nuptial chamber of the Arabian Nights, except that it had more mirrors than any eastern harem and was also incongruously enlivened by a number of paintings in the style of Pompeii. Here, finally, the doors close behind Elia and Ricardo, and they are left alone. Elia soon notices, however, that Ricardo is not taking anything in. He looks unseeingly at his surroundings, without even smiling at this grotesque parody of stage scenery. He does not see the huge bed, which hangs from the ceiling by four golden chains; he does not see the great mirror (the largest in the room) that hangs over the bed, ready to reflect their interlaced naked bodies in a few minutes time; he does not see the four plaster cupids poised around the mirror, pointing their arrows at the centre of the bed. Ricardo still says nothing. What is he thinking? wonders Elia. Perhaps that he has finally entered the shrine devoted to the most secret ceremonies; that he is now ready, after long and painful expectation, after a terrible period of trial, for the rite of initiation; that the bed (which he still shows no sign of having seen) is the sacrificial altar on which Elia will officiate in a few minutes, clad in the holy nakedness of a high priestess; and that he will leave the altar purified by the sacred fire, ready to enter without fear without shame into the world of men, having overcome every kind of fear and sorrow, every kind of adolescent anxiety and hesitation; that he will finally, irrevocably have reached adulthood ... Elia wonders for a moment whether the décor she has chosen does not contain too strong an element of parody, introducing a mocking note which is out of keeping with the sacred nature of the initiation ceremony. And now Ricardo shakes off his abstraction, realising that they have been left alone together; he looks at Elia very seriously, straight in the eye, and asks her to tell him what to do. His voice is low and not very steady, but it expresses a strong determination to see the

68

thing through. And Elia is strangely moved by the thought that she has been chosen to take him by the hand and guide him through a labyrinth of underground tunnels to the light of day. She tells him to strip and get into bed; and, as she goes off to the bathroom, she sees him beginning to go through the timid yet methodical routine of a good little boy taking off his clothes and folding them up before going to bed. When she comes back into the bedroom, his clothes are neatly folded up on a chair, his raincoat is on a coat-hanger and his shoes, each with its sock tucked into it, are standing side by side near to the bed. Now that he is naked, Ricardo looks even younger and thinner than before. Gold lamps, shaped like shells, cast a soft light over his pale, almost hairless body.

And now Elia is walking towards him, completely naked; she has never been embarrassed by her own nakedness or the nakedness of others, but she does feel constraint and discomfort at the idea of undressing or dressing (particularly dressing) with someone else there. And anyone can imagine the way in which the nymphs or priestesses of Ricardo's secret myths would take off their clothes, the strange, sophisticated strip-tease of his dreams. It is much simpler to be already naked as you approach the hero's bed, and lie down gently beside him, and softly tell him that he needn't be afraid, that there's no hurry, that everything is going to be all right; that he should keep calm, and kiss her and shut his eyes. Ricardo remains passive and trembling as she caresses him, and she knows that this is exactly what he has been longing for, the perfect realisation of the dreams of his solitary, ardent weekend. Slowly, so slowly that the movement is almost imperceptible, she must run her hands, her lips and her tongue over that young, smooth body, which is still tense with fear, though becoming less so with every minute that passes, as fear gradually gives way to desire, as

69

she continues and develops her caresses, with a light, furtive touch designed to postpone the final moment for as long as possible, to prolong to its uttermost limits this wonderful prelude, which can hardly ever be achieved with older men, who know what they want and how they want it. With lovers of that type, Elia has never been able to control the game, or to make them play it by her rules and at her pace, as she can now with Ricardo. She works very slowly, although her hands seem to have taken on a bird-like life and independent will of their own. They keep fluttering back, at shorter and shorter intervals, to the soft region between his thighs, in search of the bird imprisoned there in wild expectation of their touch, or the touch of a woman's warm body, which alone can set it free; and that expectation is now very near its breaking-point. And Elia feels something in her own body which she has never felt in the arms of more experienced lovers — a painful tingling sensation inside the warm, moist recess that is to provide the wild bird with a nest, a series of agonising stings which soon run together to form a single burning wound, the unbearable pain of a nest fiercely longing for the arrival of its irreplaceable bird ... but now the tension reaches an intolerable level for both of them, and so Elia stops caressing him with her soft hands, and slips over on top of Ricardo's body. At last the wild bird finds its nest and fulfils its destiny. Fear is forgotten, and the terror of the alien and unknown, because what has been waiting for him is not a greedy mouth full of sharp teeth, nor a fearsome cave of vampires, but a warm, softly-lined nest which has always been his destiny. The barriers gently yield before him, and vanish at his passage. Penetrating into this refuge, this nest, is a delicious experience, and the wild bird wonders how it managed to exist for so many years in agonising exile.

Elia rides feverishly on, without bridle or stirrups, mounted on Ricardo's sweaty, hairless young body, doubly excited when she hears him groan quietly, with his head down to one side and his mouth almost buried in the pillow. Speaking in a voice that she does not know, and that perhaps he too has never heard before, he asks her, between groans, if that's it, if that's all right, if the moment has come. She does not anwer him with words, but checks the to-and-fro rhythm of her movement, stops her wild ride, and presses herself against Ricardo, mouth to mouth, skin to skin, in a tight embrace; and then she rolls over, rolling him over with her since their bodies now form a single unit; and now the poet or the ape is on top and doing the riding, galloping happily along until time stops in a dizzying spasm that seems to go on forever. When it is over, Ricardo dismounts and they lie with their heads side by side on the pillow, and Elia opens her eyes and sees their two bodies reflected in the mirror. The boy's body looks very white against hers, which is bronzed by exposure to spring sunshine; and yet the two bodies have a lot in common; both look very young, very fragile, and very vulnerable as they lie there linked together in an exhausted embrace which seems to go on for ever. Elia wouldn't mind if it did ... Then Ricardo makes a curious noise, something between a satisfied purr and an excited sob, and begins to talk, in something much more like the normal voice that Elia knows so well.

Was everything all right? he asks. Did everything happen exactly as it should? Did she have a good time too? Is there some way in which it could have been even better?

He asks all this in the timid yet arrogant manner of an adolescent who has jumped his steed into the magic circle for the first time, Elia's eyes had begun to close again, but she opens them very wide at these questions, gently frees herself from his embrace, sits up in bed and explains things to him. Love, she says, is not a game with fixed rules. At least, it ought not to have fixed rules, which always degrade or

71

diminish it. Love is a free game, in which ordinary speech does not make sense. It is an open game, in which we hardly ever know what will be better or what will be worse. It is a game in which we make our way forward by guesswork and by instinct. There is therefore no possibility — not, at least, between lovers worthy of the name — of repeating an experience exactly. What has just happened between them is something that has never happened in exactly that way to Elia before. The experience is a new one not only for Ricardo, but for both of them.

The poet is delighted by this, and makes Elia repeat it four or five times — he has an infantile love of repetition. He tells her again and again that he loves her. "I love you so much, Elia . . . Elia I love you so much . . ." His voice is tender but still slightly timid. And she asks him if he is really still afraid of her. Why does his voice have that note of fear in it when he says her name?

"How can I help being afraid," he sobs, "when I know that you may disappear from one moment to another?" Elia is quite pleased to see him affected by feelings of uncertainty for a moment; today has been a day of uncertainties. Then she reassuringly tells him that it isn't like that; all things come to an end and this will too, some day, but she isn't ever going to disappear. Besides, they've only just begun, and they have lots of time left. "How much time?", he wants to know. Surprised, she replies that she doesn't know; but the poet does not accept this and finally drags from her a promise that their love will continue at least until September. It would be unbearable, he says, if she left him before September. Elia is amused and moved by his agitation, which must have its roots in his basic insecurity. There's no doubt about it, he has an extraordinary mixture of timidity and audacity, of doubt and certainty, of humility and arrogance; and then there's this frantic desire to plan everything in advance, to gain

72

control of life by reducing it to a set of rigid programmes, so that he can say things like "You must love me until September." It looks to Elia as if this beautiful, artificial, literary affair will have to go on being beautiful, artificial and literary right up to its finale — a finale foreseen four months in advance, a preplanned finale, which the two of them would then proceed to harmonise with the inevitable delicate sadness of autumn ... The ape-poet, in fact, has to be protected like a baby, wrapped up in a make-believe blanket of impossible certainties.

Elia smiles at this thought, and ruffles his dark, lank hair. She flattens her nose against his, reminding him that Eskimos are supposed to kiss like that. Lightly, ticklishly, she kisses his ears, his chest and the back of his neck; and then she lights a cigarette, which they smoke together. Elia inhales and then passes the smoke from her mouth to his — a game which delights Ricardo. He takes it up with the usual enthusiasm that both of them feel for any new game, taking the cigarette out of her hand and eagerly drawing on it himself so that he can pass the smoke to her in the same way. When it is her turn again, he is more delighted than ever with the mouthful of smoke she gives him, finally letting it drift up to the huge mirror and the plaster cupids. The poet has never smoked before, and normally cannot even stand the smell of tobacco; but now they are both smoking, as they sit cross-legged, facing each other on the enormous bed.

Everything has been so good, so correct and exciting and pleasant and agreeable, that when the poet begins to talk with passionate enthusiasm about the poetry of Ezra Pound, Elia can detect something she has noticed once or twice in the past, when they were still meeting in bars — a longing for an audience, or at least a single spectator, a wish that some third party could appreciate and perhaps immortalise this

73

exquisite scene, which is wasted on the calm, indifferent eyes of the four plaster cupids.

Clara got home rather late, as she often did nowadays — almost every night since she had taken to spending her days in Elia's flat, whether Elia was there or not, waiting for her or helping her to get ready to go out, running errands for her or answering the telephone for her, or listening to her stories; going out with her, too, from time to time, to exhibitions, to the cinema or to drink an apéritif down by the beach. Clara has always hated the street where she lived, from the first time she had seen it as a small child; she couldn't free her earliest memories from the contamination of that disagreeable feeling. She had been born there, in the same house where she still lived with her parents. She couldn't remember whether she had been two or three or four years old when she first began to notice things, but she did know that she had begun to detest her surroundings as soon as she was able to distinguish them. But now the streets seemed even more detestable, narrower, dirtier, damper. The pavements were lined with dust-bins that had lost their lids and torn plastic bags containing refuse, the contents of which had been scattered around by the sharp and expert claws of a host of hungry cats. The cats hide somewhere during the day, even Clara doesn't know where, and come out furtively, rubbing their way along the grey walls of the houses, when night begins to fall. They are ready to streak off like dark flashes of lightning, with much angry snorting and miaowing, if a car turns into the street with its headlights on; then the cats freeze for a second or two, paralysed by the sudden light, and jump aside at the last moment, swifter and angrier than ever. They also run for it when they hear the footsteps of a passer-by like Clara, although there aren't really any other passers-by like Clara, and all the cats ought to know her, and know that she is not in the least dangerous, because she is totally incapable of hurting anything or anybody. This is not the effect of a deliberate resolve not to give pain, but an inborn inability to do so — though it is difficult to imagine who she can have inherited it from. Cats are in any case the last thing she would hurt, because she has always had a special affection for them, and has fought and suffered on their behalf ever since she was a child, against her parents, her brothers, and the children in the street. Least of all could she hurt them now, when she has given Elia the title of "Little Queen of the Cats", which her friend has accepted with a smile of delight. This makes her queen not only of elegant, silky cats with long pedigrees and manicured paws, like Muslina, Elia's own Siamese, with its soft fur and huge light-blue eyes, or Persian or Angora cats, with their velvety coats of black, white or gold; she is also and above all queen of the stray cats which hide during the day and forage hungrily by night through dark, evil-smelling streets, ready to run away or put up a fight at a moment's notice. She is queen of lost cats, abandoned cats, half-wild cats or cats which come into the world because they must, without any purpose, without anyone wanting or accepting them, being born in the street or in the ruins of an abandoned house, or under a parked car; cats which will die in the street one day, while they are still quite young, without anyone caring; cats that cannot even imagine the existence of soft carpets into which you can sink your paws, or cushions of velvet or satin on which a well-fed, lazy cat can curl up in front of the fire, or linen-sheeted beds where a cat can jump up and stretch out along the beautiful, delicate body of a sleeping woman who can be approached without fear, because (although the street cats cannot understand this) there are human beings that are not dangerous. In any case, this is not strictly speaking a

75

human being, but the Queen of the Cats. She utters a little protesting moan in her sleep and pushes her hip against you with a symbolical movement which is not really meant to drive you away, although this is the Queen's very own territory and the summer is uncomfortably warm. She soon gives in and lets you go on sleeping by her side ... Those vulgar, ordinary cats, those lost cats do not even know that sunny windows exist, full of flowers and of bird-song, from which the street looks remote, alien and unreal, although for them it is the whole world, because they have never known anything else and can't even imagine it, these poor creatures of the violent, hungry night...

Or perhaps, thinks Clara, perhaps the cats do know that something different exists, perhaps they or their ancestors have occasionally heard about the Little Queen of the Cats, and perhaps they go on living and breeding in this miserable, heroic, obstinate way solely because of a hope, a legend transmitted from generation to generation as the greatest treasure of the tribe, that a day will come when the Little Queen of the Cats will come down and appear to them, or their children or their grandchildren; she will stop her snow-white coach in the middle of the horde of half-wild cats ... perhaps, thinks Clara, that's why they don't run away at once when they see a car with its headlights on coming towards them in the middle of the night; perhaps they want to make sure that it isn't the Little Queen's coach; and perhaps it's disappointment that makes them so angry when they do finally run away. Anyway, to continue with the legend of the cats, the Queen will open the door of her coach, and appear to them in her white fur coat, with her golden hair, smiling mouth and shining eyes, rather like the Snow Queen in a children's book; and then she will let the cats climb shyly on to her lap, and take them away with her to the cat's heaven ... This is after all what happened to Clara herself, which

76

proves that miracles can happen. The cats' heaven consists of a series of rooms with velvet upholstery and satin curtains, with loose rugs into which manicured paws can easily sink, with velvet cushions piled on the floor and on the sofas in front of blazing fires, with broad windows, flowerpots and birdcages, with linen sheets on the beds. Everything is smooth and easy and beautiful in those rooms, but the most important thing of all, for Clara and for the cats alike, is that the very air is impregnated with the laughter, the perfume and the voice of the Little Queen of the Cats, full of her presence even when she isn't there.

And so Clara got home late again, and found the door locked. She had to shout up to the open window — they kept it open for the summer months — a window which had some flowerpots, but no birdsong. Her mother came down and scolded her as she opened the door, and went on scolding her as she led the way upstairs, saying what she always said on these occasions; it had become a matter of routine for both of them. The landmarks Clara knew so well flittered rapidly by; the smell on the landings was even stronger and more unpleasant than the smell in the street below. Clara went into the dining-room. The table had a plastic cover over its cloth, and at it sat her father, eating his soup, with his chin almost in the plate; he did not raise his head to greet Clara or to join in her mother's reproaches, despite a hopeless attempt to enlist his support. "Just look at that girl!" she said, "and you never say anything to her!" He never intervened in the interminable quarrels of Clara's younger brothers, either — at most, he occasionally stopped eating his meal for long enough to repeat some gossip from work or some item of news from the paper. Clara sat down at the table and got on with her supper, not bothering to argue with her mother, nor to ask why her brother, who is two years younger than her, is allowed to come home any time he likes, or not come home at all, while she is expected to get home before the door is locked, leaving her earthly paradise every night at a fixed and arbitrary time to come back to the everyday reality that she hates so much. And she hates it more than ever now, much more than before; she can't stand living in this dark, dirty street, this flat with its cramped little rooms, which her mother has stuffed full of the most incredible and incongruous collection of objects which she finds and buys by the dozen in the big stores. It is at the same stores that she buys terrible clothes for Clara, who expresses her thanks in a voice trembling with dismay and puts up a heroic resistance to wearing them. Why, she wondered, are the clothes her mother buys for her so impossible, so incomparably worse than anything she has ever bought for herself? When she does finally wear these things, she invariably detects a surprised and alarmed look in the eyes of Elia.

Clara's mother devotes her mornings to housework, to getting breakfast for her sons and to preparing the mid-day meal. When she has finished with all that, and sent the woman who does the cleaning and washing-up down to the ground floor where the shop is, she helps herself to as much money as she wants out of the cash-box and goes off to the big stores. Clara's father never protests at this, and the cash-box seems to fill up again regularly day by day. So it isn't a question of money, thinks Clara, it can't be because of lack of money that everything here is so ugly and sordid; there must be some other, worse reason. . . . And so Clara's mother goes off to pursue her only hobby. She buys clothes for her daughter, her husband, her sons and herself; but she also buys statuettes of alabaster, Bulgarian ashtrays, Turkish and Greek embroideries, extraordinary kitchen utensils which are never used, and still-life pictures of two dead partridges and a plate of oranges. Clara's mother looks after the family's meals and the flat, after a fashion; she buys

78

things which make less and less sense; and she scolds her daughter. Clara reflects that her mother has never loved her; she may have loved her brothers, but never Clara herself. Her mother never gave her the love she needed, and has marked her for ever with that lack of love, that fatal deficit, that burden which she will bear for the whole of her life. It is largely that lack, that deficit, that burden which has driven her to take refuge with the Queen of the Cats.

Clara thinks all this over as she finishes her soup and starts on her plate of fish; she smiles at the reflection that the whole thing looks more and more like a contagious disease, a disastrous epidemic, because there can be no doubt that Ricardo, Elia and her own parents all received less love than they needed when they were children; and this lack of love is certainly one of the blemishes of the human race. It's rather grotesque to see them all now — overgrown waifs, arrogant foundlings, complaining that Mummy didn't love them when they were small, but using that irrevocable initial failure of love as a shield and a justification, loudly demanding love to fill the gap (though they know very well that it cannot be filled now). The whole human race is reduced to a crowd or host of lost children who haven't been able to grow up, shouting for Mummy under many different names, not knowing how to love because no one has loved them, doomed to breed new generations of loveless children in a sort of closed and interminable circle. They inspire much less respect than the animals, thinks Clara, much less respect than those half-wild cats foraging in the street, with their obstinate determination to survive — cats whose mothers loved them only until they could be weaned. It may well be that all of us adults, children and cats alike, cherish a hope that there really is a Queen of the Cats. But what about the Queen herself? wonders Clara. How is she going to cure her own basic lack of love, if she has one? Not with her husband,

79

not with the men who have probably been her lovers, and least of all with Ricardo.

Just while she is thinking about Ricardo, the telephone rings. She is surprised that he hasn't rung before. She doesn't like to get her little brother to say that she's out, because what would her mother think? In any case, she knows Ricardo would only go on ringing and ringing, ringing dozens of times until he found her at home and got her to the telephone to tell her all about it: the heroic details of this last encounter; the gradual discovery and progressive conquest of the female body, that unknown, unexplored continent, the ultimate recesses of which can never be reached; and his simultaneous discovery and mastery of his own sexuality. When Clara lifts the receiver, she hears exactly what she expected, in a detailed, implacable narrative, which does not spare her a single gesture, posture, kiss, word or caress, however much she implores him to stop, however many times she says she doesn't want to listen, and although they both know that Elia has told him not to talk to Clara about it.

(Ricardo had asked Elia to agree, and she had agreed, that he could tell his friends the whole story of his adventure and his love, since it was quite natural that the boy should want to talk to other people about his victory, and quite logical that part of the pleasure should consist in talking about it. Elia and Ricardo might find these things natural and logical, but Clara would never see them in that light. Anyway, Elia gave him full permission to say anything he liked to any of his friends, with the one exception of Clara.)

And then the detailed, implacable description broke off, as he asked her a single, excited question: "Do you know what a sixty-nine is?"

Clara felt death in her heart. It was as if the earth were heaving beneath her feet, as if Ricardo's words had drilled into her brain. She let herself fall into a chair, and dropped her hand, with the receiver, on to her lap. She could still hear the sound of Ricardo's voice, though she couldn't make out the words; but that didn't make things any better. Even without hearing or recalling his words, she could see a terrible gallery of living, moving images, pictures which she knew she wouldn't be able to blot out; she knew that nothing would ever be able to blot them out during the long, sleepless nights. She leaned her head against the wall, and clenched her jaws to control her nausea. Finally she raised the telephone to her mouth and uttered the words: "We're having supper now; I'll ring you later." She knew that those pictures were taking root in the part of her mind reserved for incurable wounds, next to the wound left by her mother's lack of love.

One thing surprises Elia ... The affair is now being conducted entirely in rooms hired by the hour, the decoration of which forms a grotesque, crazy background, which varies unexpectedly from day to day despite a persistent basic unity of style; Ricardo has now joined wholeheartedly in the game, and he is now the one who tells the boy to take them to the most fantastic and sophisticated rooms. Ricardo makes fun of the décor. Elia and he take turns at making fun of it; but she knows that for Ricardo, as for her, these rooms are a source of excitement, amusement and tremendous pleasure, because they both adore the theatrical and the artificial. Ricardo is still very abstemious in his everyday life, when Elia isn't there; but in these special circumstances he will order a *crème de menthe* with ice for Elia, and a rum cocktail for himself. When they go out together, they look with an increasingly practised eye at the contents of the shop-windows in the red-light district, and they enter the shady little shops with less and less embarrassment; for Ricardo has persuaded Elia

81

to buy, or to let him buy for her, certain items of underclothing of a far more elaborate nature than anything she has ever worn before — more elaborate, and yet perhaps more ingenuous; but in any case perfectly in keeping with the infantile perversity of the décor. These garments strike her as terribly vulgar, which may be why they amuse her; they come very near to being wholly ridiculous. The poet smiles too, though for him they evoke the historic splendours of the courtesans of eighteenth century Venice. Then they play games together like naughty children on the huge beds, some of which are hung on chains so that they rock and cradle the pair of bodies locked in combat, while others are draped in splendid scarlet hangings supported by brightly painted, mock-oriental columns, and others inspire thoughts of funerals or of betrothal ceremonies. Untiringly they play their unending twosome, with Elia laughing and pretending to struggle while Ricardo lovingly takes off her black lace brassiere, which is designed not to hide but to display her nipples — delicate, pale pink nipples, paler than ever amid the black lace, silky-smooth as the nipples of a young girl, nipples which stir Clara deeply every time she catches a glimpse of them under the shower or in the bath and which seem to drive Ricardo right out of his mind. Then he takes off her pants, which are embroidered with hearts or birds strategically arranged around a clearly marked central point. Next come her garters, black to match her brassiere, and decorated with sequins or ribbons the colour of amaranth. Ricardo and Elia talk and laugh almost all the time as they experiment with unheard-of caresses and strange positions, which sometimes leads to extraordinary heights of pleasure, and sometimes run up against physical impossibility and collapse amid gales of laughter. Then they sip their *crème de menthe* and their rum cocktail. Ignoring Elia's protests, Ricardo slides his icy glass across her warm belly and over her breasts, and then warms them up again with his kisses. They light a cigarette, and pass the smoke from mouth to mouth, and talk about music or poetry; everything is so pleasant, so delicate, so natural and so charming, as the two children innocently play a game which may happen to be forbidden, so that Elia knows there is no room here for the intoxication of agony or ecstasy — the intoxication that leaves her head spinning, her limbs scattered far and wide, with a cruel claw piercing her throat and breasts, and a terrible chill of cold steel in her belly. It's not that sort of affair; or, to be more exact, it was that sort of affair only for a couple of days, from the Friday when she made her promise to the Monday when she led him along the dark tunnel to the altar of sacrifice and initiation, out of the dark and into the light. That very morning, as they smoked their cigarette and laughed and chattered, the affair changed into something pleasant, agreeable and gentle; there was a little intoxication about it, but only a very little. Elia also knows that it's the same for her poet, that this isn't the great love of Ricardo's life either. It's a delightful apprenticeship in which he learns what love will be for him later on, if he's lucky. It's a starting-point from which he'll be able to set off confidently after other women or girls. Clara thinks that it's sacrilegious of the poet to make use of Elia in this way, and terribly insulting that he should presume to lay down a time-limit for his love-affair with her; but Elia does not agree with Clara, because she knows that she is also making use of Ricardo, using him as a shield against anxiety and fear, against boredom and nothingness; nor does Elia regard herself as being really in love with him . . . The thing that surprises Elia is this. In the hired rooms where they meet, they talk and talk until they are exhausted; though Ricardo is never really exhausted when it comes to talking or to making love to her. They talk about art, history, politics or artistic fashions, sitting cross-legged on fantastic beds, surrounded by cigarette smoke and the tinkle of ice in their drinks. They talk and talk untiringly, before, after and even during the act of love. This makes it rather strange that Ricardo has rung her up today to ask her to meet him in one of the bars where they used to meet before, "so that we can talk."

She finds him drinking a coca-cola without any gin or rum in it. Alcohol is evidently only for erotico-literary occasions. He greets her with unsmiling gravity. On the table is a slim volume of verse, though Elia is sure he does not want to talk about poetry today. Elia is both gratified and amused to notice that he has now learned exactly the right way to greet her. Quite the advanced student in the art of love, with his burning eyes, his moist lips which plant a long-long kiss on her lips, and another on her cheek, and then another on her neck, while his hands reach out towards her, touch her, embrace her and sit her down at his side; finally they seek out and grasp her own hands. As they sit together, Ricardo gives her a long, intense gaze, and softly repeats her name over and over again, because he knows that she likes it, or because he has decided that she likes it, or because she once told him that she liked it without quite knowing why. He is nice today, and Elia has a pleasant feeling in her heart, a faint, agreeable emotion that has nothing dangerous about it, she thinks, because, like everything else in this charming story, it is quite easy to keep under control.

Ricardo has arranged to meet her in a bar today because he has something important to tell her, so important that he evidently needs a different décor, saner, less theatrical, more neutral scenery. When he has finished repeating her name like an incantation, he adopts a slightly more serious expression — he is not frightened of anything now, because he knows that she is going to love him until September — and he begins to talk about Clara. He talks in a very detailed and

84

precise manner, with interminable, systematic, obsessive exactness. Elia reflects that this aspect of his character, like a steamroller driven by syllogisms, is not new to her. He was like that the day when they first got to know each other (or rather the day on which she got to know him, since apparently he knew her from an earlier occasion; strange to think that we can exist intensely for someone of whose existence we are still unaware.) He was also the same on the day when he told her that he had fulfilled their agreement and fallen in love with her . . . It is a remarkable thing that strict logic, applied with extreme rigour to human beings, so often breaks down into insanity. There must be a mistake, a catch in his argument somewhere; but she tries in vain to see where the catch lies, or where the mistake lurks. Perhaps there are no mistakes or catches, but in that case she can't discover why Ricardo's argument should completely disarm her and overcome her resistance, without in any way convincing her that he is right. His argument may be objective and brilliant, with the chilly strength of a math-emtical equation or the structural analysis of a poem, but why should she accept it against her better judgement? Ricardo insists that she should answer a simple question with a simple yes or no; but this, too, is strangely difficult — perhaps because the question is too simple, too absolute, to be answered briefly at all. "Do you love Clara?" he asks, as if love were something well defined, something you either have or don't have, something you give or withhold, like money in your purse; as if the word "love" (like the word "orchid") did not cover an almost infinite number of varieties. There are as many different species of love as there are people in the world who have loved, love or will love. It's rather like what they used to tell us at school about archangels, thinks Elia with a smile as she silently listens to the development of Ricardo's argument. Each archangel belongs to a category of his own, and it is useless to try to classify them according to a common denominator . . . In point of fact, the number of kinds of love is not equivalent to the number of lovers, but much larger, because it is most unlikely that an individual will experience only one kind of love in the course of his life. There is therefore no end to the variety of different and often irreconcilable feelings which we arbitrarily lump together under this facile label of "love", which explains nothing, being too wide and too vague to retain any precise meaning. Elia reflects that the question is much simpler for Ricardo, and would be much simpler for Clara too, if she were to be consulted on the subject, because Clara also sees love as a definite object that either is or isn't there, like a pimple on your nose or a shower of rain. There is no room in Clara's scheme of things for half-measures like blackheads or Scotch mists.

Clara loves Elia, the poet loves Elia, the poet used to love Clara, Clara never loved the poet, now the poet has stopped loving Clara, they don't love each other but they both love Elia . . . And what about you? asks Ricardo. Do you love Clara?

Elia realises that she has got to answer. She must make him understand her, she must stop him talking on this primitive, barbarous level about absolute reality. What a nuisance the very young can sometimes be! Elia feels as if she has been approached by a savage — or perhaps a pair of savages, since it is possible that Clara has something to do with it — and asked whether she can bring the god of fire down into the room. There's no point in trying to explain about electricity; you just say yes, because what they really want to know is whether you can turn on the light. At the same level of relative truthfulness, Elia now says no, she doesn't love her.

The thought that she did not love Clara has been floating vaguely in Elia's mind for some time, but she had never expressed it in words before, even to herself. Now that she had put it into words, it took on a much more definite quality and acquired a new degree of plausibility and truth. It became a certainty when she uttered the words "I don't love her." (That may be why Clara herself had never asked that question, for fear that Elia would say "I don't love you" and that the words would become true as soon as they were spoken.)

Ricardo seems oddly surprised by Elia's reply, and says: "Then why . . ." and Elia is surprised in her turn by the degree of ingenuity that is revealed by Ricardo's reaction. The question that Ricardo has left half finished can only be "Why did you let her go on loving you, if you knew that you couldn't love her?" There are plenty of reasons. Because Clara is persistent, attentive and sweet, very sweet sometimes; because she has huge, beautiful dark eyes in a small, pale face; because she is so young, so movingly young, while Elia, now in her thirties, is or thinks she is on the point of beginning to leave youth behind her; because Elia needs an intoxicant to free her from apathy, boredom and anguish, and it is becoming harder and harder for her to obtain relief, so that she finds herself desperately, hopelessly searching for it in the most unlikely places, places where she knows she won't even find a temporary substitute for what she wants; or because she wanted (as she often does) a fresh audience for the stories which she remembers, embroiders or invents, and Clara is, as Ricardo is the first to admit, a really wonderful listener, attentive and sensitive, respectful and receptive, always ready to come in at the right moment with just the question that the speaker needs to set him off on the next stage of his story. Another reason is that Elia needs a mirror; she has no self-confidence (though Ricardo does not know this), and she leaves other people to assign a value to her so that she can tell where she stands; but the unwelcome, treacherous image that unexpectedly greets her in the ordinary mirrors of hall and bathroom fills her with surprise, suspicion and disgust. The best mirror is the one provided by Clara; in it Elia sees herself as she used to dream of being when she was still a child, as she now knows she will never really be. Clara brings together all Elia's lost opportunities from the past and projects them into a future which does not really exist, but which they nevertheless elaborate together, as Elia lets herself become an accomplice in the farcical comedy . . . Or again, perhaps it's because the weather has been so hot during this long spring, and the days are so long; these intolerable evenings when it's still light at nine o'clock depress Elia, and frighten her too.

Or perhaps Elia let the thing go on, allowed the story to continue, because there were moments when she thought that she really did love Clara in a way, or could at least hope to be able to love her later on; and it was mainly during those moments — not exclusively, but mainly then — that she gave the girl some encouragement. There was no doubt about the result — Clara declared her feelings and burnt her boats at once, taking a step from which retreat was almost impossible — all without asking Elia if she loved her, or even apparently contemplating the possibility that her love might be returned.

The thought that Clara is capable of loving her like that, capable of that sort of devotion, fills Elia with rage and envy, and with a bitter conviction that however things turn out Clara will have the best of it. Clara will probably have all the pain, or most of it; but she also possesses an abundance of that much-desired intensity of the imagination and the senses which Elia knows to be out of her reach, although she would gladly give the rest of her life for a small share of it . . . How *dare* this young brat ask for the additional gift of happiness or reciprocated love, or put Ricardo up to asking for them on her behalf, when she already has the plentitude of ecstatic intoxication? Anyway, Clara began to haunt Elia's flat, and to worship her with the hopeless adoration of an alley cat; she installed herself in the flat with the unchanging persistence, the unfailing availability of a piece of furniture.

As she explained all this to Ricardo, Elia felt that she had come to a shaky part of the story, and began to feel just a little guilty. Her voice took on an emphatic tone, which revealed her wish to justify herself, though what she said was not exactly a moral justification of the kind that Ricardo seemed to be expecting. Clara, she said, was so lonely and vulnerable, so uncomfortable in her surroundings, so much the outsider with her family, her home and the part of the city where she lived, and so ignorant (in spite of her secondary education and her first year at the university); and at the same time she was so malleable and so willing to learn that teaching her was a wonderful experience. Elia had never been able to teach her own children anything; they had been educated for good or ill by their environment, by the constant presence of friends and relations, of their father, of nannies, schoolmasters and schoolmistresses; they had never been so dependent on her as Clara, so loving, so much in need of her help, so ready to learn. And so it was a wonderful experience to teach Clara, and to see how she learnt things immediately, often without a word having been said. She taught her how to lay a table, how to use knives and forks correctly, how to make tea, and how to behave in the theatre. She even taught her how to do her hair and how to dress, leaving aside the extraordinary monstrosities which her mother bought for her or taking them back to be exchanged for something better; for Clara's mother was still buying clothes for her from time to time in the big stores, together with alabaster statuettes and wickerwork boxes from the Philippines or Japan.

Ricardo nodded understandingly: it is deeply satisfying to play Pygmalion with a pupil as quick and intelligent and as pretty as Clara. He too had played the same game though in quite a different field — Elia's lessons being concerned with more trivial matters, while he had concentrated on the more serious and difficult disciplines of criticism and scholarship. Clara is, in fact, to some extent the product of their joint efforts. Elia can now see that Ricardo is not after all concerned with the moral side of the question; he probably shares her basic passion for playing vicious games, her need to understand and live her life in terms of games and vice. There is something else of which Ricardo must be intuitively aware, although neither he nor Elia has so far put it into words. It is that Elia, although knowing perfectly well that she cannot really love Clara, has from time to time played at loving her, because Ricardo and Clara have somehow become characters in the same story, players in the same match, so that there would be something incomplete, unbalanced or out-of-key if the match had not become in some sense a threesome. At this point the poet sets his terrible syllogistic steamroller in motion again, rumbling irrestistibly on towards a crazy conclusion; if Elia finds the girl interesting and attractive and in some ways helpful, if Elia has already more than once considered the possibility of loving her, why doesn't she pursue the matter to its logical finale? Why, he asks in his most serious voice, doesn't Elia do the same with and for Clara as she has already done with and for him?

How literary and artificial this whole story is, thinks Elia, from its beginning as a fable of the jungle to its fated end amid the splendours of autumn! She again has the feeling that the affair *must* take the principle of symmetry to its logical conclusion. In his cool, objective, impersonal way, Ricardo is indicating the necessity of introducing an additional feature, an extra window or cornice, to ensure that

90

the neo-classical façade does not lose its perfect, balanced harmony ... And what a banal, artificial harmony it is anyway! Elia is conscious of a feeling of shock, withdrawal and protest in her innermost being; she dimly feels that there is something wrong with Ricardo's reasoning; she has a premonition that a vital mistake or a trap is somehow involved; a hidden danger is definitely lying in wait, but for whom? — for herself? — for the three of them? — or just for Clara? And yet, in spite of all these forebodings, Elia knows that she is defeated in advance, defeated by the inexorable rigour of the argument which he lays out before her like a series of moves at chess. The possible consequences of the initiative under consideration are the following: a) Clara does not enjoy the experience but nevertheless remains in love with Elia, b) Clara does get her pleasure from the experience and falls more deeply in love with Elia then ever, c) Clara derives no pleasure from what happens in bed and loses interest in Elia, d) ... but there's no point going on with this, no point in even listening to the words, because Elia knows she can't resist Ricardo's untiring persistence, his unconquerable obstinacy. Elia finds herself less and less capable of identifying exactly where the trap or the mistake is hidden in this thicket of verbiage. She knows very well that there can only be one end to all the points listed, all the various possibilities examined, and that is victory for Ricardo and defeat for her. One reason for her defeat is her own love of the game, her own passion for moving the pieces, her own ridiculous desire to play God, and to convince herself of her importance (or perhaps merely of her existence) by dint of interfering in other people's lives, which is one of the most dangerous, and also one of the most effective, ways in which Elia can escape from her boredom and inactivity. Elia believes, however, or would like to believe, that the first and principal reason for her defeat is contained in the internal

91

logic of their story, a story which has been bipolar in its original conception and bipolar in its development. Clara has always been there, as an unseen presence, at her meetings with Ricardo; and similarly Ricardo has always been there during her conversations with Clara. The idea which Ricardo is now putting forward so explicitly and with such a wealth of logic sounds quite familiar to Elia, like something said and accepted long ago, like the words without which a sonnet would be incomplete, or the notes without which a symphony would lose its form, or the sequences without which a film would lose its meaning. What the poet proposes can almost be regarded as a stylistic necessity, as the finishing touch demanded by a story which, being their story, must be absolutely perfect.

"Why don't you stay the night?" says Elia. "There's nobody here, and I don't like being alone in the house." She says this lightly, unemphatically, almost indifferently, as if it were something quite natural, something which had often happened before. Clara feels as if she were dreaming, as if her last link with reality had broken, as if the last rope that moored her boat to the quayside had parted. She is desperately afraid of waking up, being quite clear in her mind that she is dreaming, and that the only guarantee of her happiness is to be found in the fragile logic of dreams. She lets the waves rock her as she floats away, a buoy that has slipped its caable, a freely drifting boat, floating towards the high seas or towards the stars. Sunk in her dream, she hardly knows what she is doing as she dials her home number, without a trace of the fear she would have felt in the waking world. Clara's mother answers; but Clara hardly hears what she says, does not even listen in fact. Clara's voice is steadier than you might expect, as she goes straight into the story that she has

92

discussed and prepared in advance with Elia, who is smilingly supporting her in her little peccadillo, her enjoyable
subterfuge, as she says: "Elia's not feeling very well and has
asked me to stay the night and look after her." Her mother's
reply is most unexpected, but Clara absorbs it without
surprise. "I'd rather you stayed there," she says, "than have
you wandering about the streets at heavens knows what hour
of the morning." So that's what miracles are like, thinks
Clara, they're quite simple, really. She remembers something
that happened a long time ago, though she's not sure she
isn't making some of it up, as she tells Elia how one night,
years ago, she'd been asked to spend the evening with a
schoolfriend, a tall girl with a round face and long, blond
hair; and how, when it got dark, her friend's mother filled up
the big bath-tub with its feet like dragon's claws and gave
them both a bath in the warm water, with little celluloid fish
and boats floating among the soap-suds. Then she took the
two children out of the bath and dried them with a huge, soft,
pink towel; and then she didn't dress Clara up again in her
dismal, everyday clothes, her ordinary shoes — the protective
uniform of a schoolgirl, in fact — and send her home, but
gave her a suit of pyjamas like her friend's. They were white
winceyette pyjamas, with an apple embroidered in red and
green in the middle of the chest. (Now that Clara comes to
think of it, she seems to remember that her friend's pyjamas
didn't have an apple embroidered on them, but a golden sun
with eyes and a nose and a mouth and lots of rays pointing in
all directions.) Then her friend's mother laughed and said
"You're going to stay here with us tonight!"; and Clara
thought that it couldn't be true, that it couldn't really
happen, least of all without warning like that. She couldn't
really be going to spend the night in that blue-and-white flat,
with its teddy bears and black-eyed dolls, and go to sleep in a
nice little bed with a crochet-work coverlet, holding hands

with the prettiest, blondest girl in the whole school. "I can't," she said, "my mother won't let me." Clara looked up at her friend's mother, who was so different from her own mother, so like the lovely mothers you read about in stories, just as that little flat was like an illustration from a children's book, and her friend was like the prettiest of all enchanted princesses. (As she tells the story, Clara can feel it becoming more and more of an invention and less and less of a memory.) And then, with an air of great complicity, that laughing, affectionate mother said: "Don't worry; I'm just going to ring her up." Clara stood there trembling, with her heart in her mouth, sure that her mother would say no, sure that it was not to be. But the same thing happened on that distant, half-legendary night as has just happened now: against all expectation, her mother said yes, and it did happen. Then as now, Clara was suddenly free of everything she hated, but only for one night, because her friend's mother never asked her to stay the night again; in fact Clara isn't sure that she ever went to her friend's home to play again. That must have been because the other girl changed schools — and how could you expect a girl like that to stay at a school like the one Clara went to? — and she never saw her again. Clara really can't remember this bit, and is probably making it up; but she does definitely remember that she got away for one night from the dark, ugly bedroom she shared with her grandmother, which smelled of damp, of cabbage, of dirty clothes and of medicines for the elderly. Clara's bed was much too big and much too cold; and from it she could hear the harsh, bitter, strident voices of her parents, interminably arguing about sordid questions, generally concerned with money, though the real object of their discussion was, and still is, not to find a solution to a problem, but merely to give vent to their mutual bitterness. They used to quarrel in the kitchen and quarrel in front of the television, and stop quarrelling with each other only when it was time to quarrel with their son for coming home too late, as he often did even then, when he was still a kid.

Clara goes on with her story, remembered or imaginary, and tells Elia how, just for that one night and never again, she wore those pretty, comfortable pyjamas, and slept in a bed which looked as if it came out of a doll's house and was exactly the right size for her, and she wasn't lonely any more, because her friend was there beside her in an identical bed. (There must have been another child in the family who was away for some reason, and that was probably why her friend's mother had asked Clara to stay, so that she wouldn't be lonely.) Clara remembers how her friend's blond locks spread out over the pillow, and remembers how the little girl smiled and reached out her hand, and they lay there holding hands, giggling and whispering, exchanging confidences, almost all the night. Nobody came to scold them, and they must finally have dropped off to sleep at dawn.

What a long time it's been since then . . . What a long time. And now Elia has said "I don't like being alone in the house; why don't you stay?" and her mother has said "I'd rather you stayed there than wandered about in the streets." It is as if these words mark the beginning of a dream, or the renewal of Clara's old dream; as if miracles were again becoming the order of the day. It is as if Elia had already known about that far-off night (which Clara herself had almost forgotten), and had possessed the key to its mystery. Elia is excited and happy, as Clara has never seen her before, laughing gaily with exactly the same casual, carefree expression as Clara's hostess on that earlier occasion — looking rather like her, too, with the same auburn hair and white hands, and the same air of happily starting something slightly naughty. Elia takes Clara into the bathroom, and turns on the taps. This bath-tub has no dragon's feet and is not painted white;

everything in Elia's bathroom is black or pink. As the water runs in, Elia adds a thick, scented bubble-bath, and whisks it up into a sea-green foam. Then she undresses Clara, who resists and smiles and gives way. She puts her in the bath, and passes the sponge slowly over her breasts, round her neck, down her back, and over her belly and legs; all with great attention to detail, as if she were really bathing a child. Elia bustles in and out of the room, fetches a towel, and helps Clara to dry her hair and her back. Then she gives her a nightdress of fine white cambric, almost transparent, with blue ribbons round the neck and sleeves. Although Clara has seen Elia wear it once or twice before, this garment is as much outside Clara's normal scheme of things as the winceyette pyjamas with the apple embroidered on the chest had been on the previous occasion. Elia also lends her a blue house-coat and a pair of slippers. And then, still with the same air of a little girl doing something naughty, she leads Clara to the dining-room. And there on the table, among white roses and lilies, is a sort of crazy picnic — Elia has been opening tins in her kitchen and getting in sweets from the pastry shop down the street. There's lobster in white wine, there are hare and pheasant pâtés, strawberry and raspberry tarts covered in cream, marrons glacés, mint chocolates and liqueur chocolates; and now Clara is laughing too, because this is a fantastic, fairy-tale meal, specially devised for a good little girl, or for an affectionate kitten, by the Little Queen of the Cats. They sample the dishes and laugh and drink a very light, very cold wine. Clara can't really swallow any food; she always has this difficulty when she is with Elia, but what does it matter whether you eat or not if the whole thing is a dream? Clara drinks her wine and laughs and purrs and curls up on the sofa very close to Elia. Elia puts her arm round Clara's shoulder and kisses her slowly, lightly; she kisses her closed eyes, her burning cheeks, her mouth, the back of her neck,

96

her ears, and along the top of the nightdress, just above her trembling breasts. "You're a bit drunk," says Elia, "we're both a bit drunk. Do you like it?" Clara nods; she can't get a word out, but she nods, thinking that never in her whole life has she ever liked anything so much or felt so happy, in spite of feelings of embarrassment, in spite of the terrible fear that she is going to wake up. For the first time in her life, she feels that there may be a place for her somewhere in this crazy world, a warm corner in this beastly universe where she can curl up and rest . . . And it isn't true that either of them is even slightly drunk; or if they are, it's not with wine, but with that particular intoxication that comes from a mixture of liqueur chocolates and dreams.

Clara lets Elia help her to her feet, though she could probably get up perfectly well by herself, she lets Elia support her and half-carry her to the huge bed in the pink bedroom. She remains passive as Elia very carefully puts her to bed, swinging her feet up on to the mattress, and arranging the pillow comfortably under her head. Then Clara can hear Elia moving around the room in the dark, because she's switched off the lamp and there's only a little light coming through the bathroom door. Clara waits as she waited that other time, all those years ago, her body trembling and her heart in her mouth; but this time she's sure she's going to die if Elia really comes and lies down at her side. If Elia, instead of giving her a good-night kiss and going away, really comes and lies down at her side she knows she will die. She lies there shivering from head to foot, her eyes closed. She is full of such tremendous desire and such total confusion, fear and shame that she would like to be able to make time stop for a few moments, to give herself a few minutes to recover and get her breath back; but Elia has already come over to the bed and lain down at her side, and put her arm round her shoulders, and pulled her very gently towards her. "Dear Clara," she says, "why are you trembling? What are you afraid of?" And she rocks her in her arms and coos to her as if Clara were really a little girl. Presently the trembling stops and the fear ebbs away, and slowly, very slowly, Clara finds that she can breathe again. And then, only then, Elia holds her a little more tightly and whispers "My pretty one, my little girl, my beauty . . ." And they stay there together like that, silent and motionless for a long time. Clara isn't sure which of them moves first, but suddenly the two of them are pressed close together, face to face, with their legs interlocked and their bodies moving in a smooth rhythm which is also the rhythm of Elia's words. Although infinitely sweet and soothing to both of them, these words have something secret and terrible about them because they come from an Elia that Clara has never known before, except perhaps in dreams; an Elia that neither husband nor lovers — and least of all Ricardo — can ever have even glimpsed. For weeks past, Clara has been depressed and tormented by jealousy, choked by its bitter taste; but now that feeling dies peacefully away, because this is a new Elia — not the easily-smiling goddess, not the casual, loose-living woman of the world, and not the enterprising, successful amorist given over to sophisticated caresses and perverse disguises. It is none of these that now holds Clara in her arms; it is an infinitely tragic and lonely child, an unlucky woman trying to extract herself and her dreams from the swamp, who embraces and comforts not just Clara, but all the fear and loneliness in the world. The Queen of the Cats has never seemed so small, delicate and vulnerable to Clara as she does now, while the love that has been dammed up in Clara's heart for months past bursts its banks and fills her being with sorrowful compassion, with a pure and ardent desire to protect Elia. It becomes uncertain which of them is comforting the other from what unknown fears, which of them is rocking the other in her arms as you rock a

98

child to stop it crying and send it to sleep. They caress each other as carefully as you'd stroke a wounded animal, as tenderly as you'd touch a new-born baby; until Elia's hand slips gently into the warm, moist space between Clara's thighs. Clara lies very still for a few moments of shock and dismay; then she moans softly and presses herself more tightly against Elia's body, stretches out, and finally goes to sleep like a good little girl.

Ricardo's mother has gone out — probably to the church, to say her rosary or to attend the usual novena, thinks Ricardo, though this is pure conjecture, a mere literary supposition. He could easily find out if he wanted to, but he doesn't know, because he isn't interested and doesn't ask, where his mother goes in the afternoon, when she sets out from the flat, very erect and tidy in her black dress, as she has today. She may be going to the church, or she may just as easily be going shopping, or to visit her cousin or a friend. But in that case, thinks Ricardo, continuing with his reverie, the people she visits must have an invalid in the house, or have recently had a death in the family. It would be much less logical, and much more boring, if his mother were to visit friends or relations with the sole object of passing a pleasant half hour with them, exchanging gossip, and deriving pleasure or even amusement from her outing. In the same way, if his mother turned out to have gone to the shops, her shopping could hardly follow the same pattern as the shopping of Elia or Clara's mother, with the successive and mounting pleasures of looking for what you want, finding it and taking possession of it. If Ricardo's mother goes shopping, it must be to make a few necessary, sensible purchases, with nothing spontaneous or enjoyable about them; and this isn't only or even mainly because there is very little money in the house.

Anyway, Ricardo's mother has gone out to an unknown destination, as she has on so many other afternoons, in her black dress spotted with white flowers — a semi-mourning dress, Ricardo remembers, and that detail does seem logical and appropriate to him, although he's not sure in whose honour she is wearing it, and can't imagine how his mother would ever stop mourning once she had started. A diamond and aquamarine brooch is pinned to the lapel, near her left shoulder, and her face is lightly dusted with rice powder which no one uses nowadays. There is an unpleasant expression about the corners of her mouth, as if she were meditating a cruel, private sarcasm, or some silent act of revenge; or as if she were on the point of spitting out a long accumulation of bitterness. Or that expression may be all that is left of a grimace originally used to compress and conceal her ardent desires (assuming that she ever had any) within pursed lips. It may be a final trace of former warmth and passion in that neat, upright figure, which is now facing the first afflictions of old age, facing them with a disagreeable expression, but without complaint. She is beginning to limp a little from the arthritis that has already deformed her hands. She is confronting old age in the same detached manner in which she has long confronted loneliness — a loneliness which she has voluntarily accepted and prolonged, if she didn't voluntarily create it in the first place. Ricardo is not sure whether it was by his mother's choice that love has taken on such a remote and insipid character for her, so that her affections, like her shopping, are limited to the necessary and the sensible. Something in her, whether it be religious conviction or some secret defensive instinct, has always led her to keep a certain distance between herself and any human being. (A dog or a cat, thinks Ricardo with a smile, would have even less chance with his mother, who finds even birds too passionate and too emotionally disturbing, and finds a safe

100

outlet for her feelings in the impenetrable world of potted plants.) She has always maintained a certain distance between herself and her awkward young son, who everybody says is so intelligent, and she believes it, though it's impossible to tell whether or not she feels flattered, whether or not she feels happy to hear it . . . So awkward, so clever, and such a good boy, really; she undoubtedly loves him very much; and yet never once, thinks Ricardo bitterly, never once during childhood, boyhood or the present beginnings of manhood, has he found a welcoming comfort in her lap, at her bosom or in her arms. How often had his affectionate, spontaneous gestures been nipped in the bud by the uncomfortable, astonished, alarmed look in his mother's eyes! She has very large, pale blue eyes, with a mineral quality about them. They were the most beautiful and also the most chilling feature of a mother who you felt ought to be a standing on an altar like a wax image, surrounded by white flowers, so that you could kneel before her and pray. Such a brave, unselfish woman, so given up to self-sacrifice, so strong against adversity, so stern with herself and her family! Her family, in the strict sense, consisted of Ricardo and Ricardo alone. Having been cast out of her womb once and for all, Ricardo was never allowed to act out his nostalgia for that lost refuge by laying his cheek against that sunken belly, between the projecting hip-bones. He was never allowed to put an ear to that body, which, pale and withered as it was, might still vibrate with a precious, forgotten music from which a child could draw comfort and escape for a few moments from the full harshness of exile. Other mothers might be like that, anyway . . .

How well she has confronted the years of loneliness and poverty, with what dignity and integrity she has presided over the inexorable decline of what was once a well-to-do family! (Ricardo suspects that the family was never quite so prosperous as she now makes out.) How bravely she has put up with the sarcastic or spiteful smiles of the neighbours and the impertinence of the portress. And for a few moments Ricardo forgets his bitterness, as his mother comes in, leans over him and kisses him on the cheek, with a kiss so aseptic and formal as not to be a kiss at all, but a negative image of what a kiss should be ... Ricardo forgets his bitterness against his mother, forgets the unending record of daily grievances that seperates them; for a few moments he even forgets the scenes he has been imagining, as he sits at his desk with an open Latin grammar in front of him — scenes in which the docile, interlaced, superimposed figures of Clara and Elia play the main parts. As so often before, Ricardo is overawed by the stiff, impeccable figure of his mother, who always looks as if she were going to church whatever her real destination may be. For a moment he seems to see the faint, dark halo of a mantilla round her head, as she used to wear it in the old days, with the ends pinned to her lapel by the diamond and aquamarine brooch. It is in fact quite a long time since she stopped going out in her mantilla. She had been the last woman in the neighbourhood to give it up, and had felt the same annoyance as a general who finds that custom no longer permits him to wear his medals and his orders when he goes out in society. But even like this, with no mantilla, or rather with the impalpable ghost of a mantilla, there is something very impressive about this tall, strong-boned woman, with mineral-blue eyes brighter and colder than her aquamarines, and her obstinate refusal to use a stick despite her increasing lameness, just as, for years past, she has refused every kind of support, help or comfort. She has devoted the last fifteen years, the best years of her life, to her son and to the church, ever since the death of Ricardo's father, whom he can hardly remember. "Fifteen years of self-denial and sacrifice!" thinks Ricardo. The word

102

"sacrifice", in any context, however inappropriate, always makes Ricardo think of his mother, and then his expression hardens and his face grows dark. This has been self-denial and sacrifice without love, or at least without any expression of love. His mother's soul was too exalted — or perhaps not exalted enough? — to find room for ordinary tenderness or affection, for merely human feelings or for the warmth of life. During the years before Ricardo's great rebellion, when he still went to Mass with her every Sunday, he used to see her going up to the altar for the eucharist, kneeling to kiss images, pedestals, vestments, rings and relics; but no look of joy or comfort ever crossed her face even there. There can be nothing agreeable or consoling about religious observance for a stern-minded general who has lost his medals but not his honour, or for a wax madonna wearing the ghost of a mantilla for a halo. Religion and motherhood seem to be the two things that have kept her going; but at the same time they have been two heavy burdens on her back, to be borne without faltering but also without pleasure. And so now she kisses Ricardo on the cheek without faltering and without pleasure. For a few moments Ricardo feels a real admiration for her; but this is followed by irritation with her for being like that and with himself for responding with secret admiration and respect; and he revenges himself with a malevolent smile. "Whatever are you laughing at?" asks his mother, slightly disconcerted; but Ricardo says nothing and continues to smile. His mother shrugs her shoulders and leaves the room without asking again. Just as she has given up so many other things in her life, she gives up the attempt to understand this ultimately incomprehensible son. For Ricardo is not going to explain to her that he is making an attempt — possibly his last attempt — to exorcise his old fears, and the unchanging anguish that has plagued him for so long, which afflicts him with everyone he meets, but most

103

of all with her; that feeling of guilt which has no real justification, but which his armoury of syllogisms cannot destroy though it was primarily with this object that he set the armoury up in the first place. Ricardo has always found it much easier to convince other people with his dialectic skills than to convince himself . . . Anyway, Ricardo is making this attempt, this probably last attmpt, to exorcise those fears and that anguish — emotions which he is ashamed of feeling, emotions which his mother has unwittingly fostered, and of which she is the symbol. He is exorcising them by the simple childish method of imagining his mother's stiff, upright body, a body which can't possibly have any warm nooks or regions of agreeable softness, a long, thin, unhealthily white body, dressed up in the transparent red nightdress which he bought yesterday for Elia, and which is now hidden in the bottom drawer of his desk, under a layer of books and papers. What a contrast there would be between that worn, thin flesh, through which blue veins can be seen, and sharp bones pressing outwards to the skin, and the breasts which he imagines as limp and drooping, though in fact his mother has almost no bosom at all. (Can it be that no one, not even his father, has ever played with them?) Perhaps her chest would be flat, or even hairy, like a general's; her hips are wide, her belly fallen in, her pubic region with its thin covering of greying hair . . . what a contrast between all that, which he imagines or invents without ever having seen it, and the light, cheerful, transparent garment, which came to life and took on three-dimensional shape for him as soon as he noticed it in the show-case. In his mind's eye, he could see it being entered, occupied and filled out by Elia's shapely, luxuriant body; for Elia is a *fausse maigre*, a woman of apochryphal slimness, as he often tells her. Elia does look slim, slim as a boy or a very young girl, when you see her elegant, remote figure slip past in the street or in a drawing-room; but in the

104

bedroom, when she undresses or when you undress her —
Ricardo has overcome his reserve and his inhibitions enough
to be able to take Elia's clothes off, put them on again, and to
disguise her in various ways — as the clothes come off, her
body seems to blossom forth into unexpected, rich curves,
warm and sumptous. Her breasts, her legs and her belly form
a luxurious refuge where you can curl up and go to sleep; her
pink nipples, smooth as a young girl's, are as sweet as honey;
and then there's something warm, moist, clinging and fragrant, like a flower in the marsh where she wandered so long,
like a nest, like the lair of an animal, something which takes
away all fear. For Ricardo it is a starting-point, a platform
from which he can launch himself on a new adventure, taking
with him in enhanced form his ambition and his anger, his
frustrations and his secret envies, as he sets out to the
conquest of a world by which he has too long felt himself to
be ignored, despised or mocked, a world which he at once
feared, hated and desired. That world has begun to open up
before him like a ripe fruit, and the first stage of his
triumphant path has been the comfortingly mature yet
eternally youthful body of Elia.

Ricardo thinks of Elia, and then of Clara — or does he
think of Clara first and then of Elia! The two female images
are becoming ever more closely linked in his imagination,
melting into a single figure, combining to compensate and
pacify him for all the humilitation and all the accumulated
rancour, for all the pain and all the insults of an unhappy
past. This single, joint image of the two women may well
mark for him the beginning of a future without fear . . . That
was — and had to be — the essence of his initiation. And for
that initiation it had to be Elia and no one else, not a woman
encountered by chance or by accident, but Elia herself, the
only possible choice, not only because she is clever and pretty
and civilised and sensitive but above all because she is

intensely different and intensely desirable — desired not only by Ricardo himself, but also (and this is equally important) by other men; and this is what makes her such a splendid symbol.

"Give me a point of support . . ." Ricardo remembers her saying, in a soft, tender, laughing singsong, a little tipsy after two *crèmes de menthe*, as she flipped his organ gently between two fingers, squeezed it with a firm, warm hand, pressed it between her breasts, stropped it against her erected nipples, and finally slid it into her mouth; her teeth were like the sheathed claws of an affectionate cat, and her tongue moved in an intense, vibrant application, which owed as much to natural virtuosity as to acquired technique — "Give me a point of support and I will move the world!" she says, as she flips, squeezes, presses, strops, licks and sucks, making him cry out aloud with pleasure and desire; until finally he sits up and grasps her firmly by the shoulders, and pulls her up on top of his body, in a strong, slow movement, dragging the points of her hard nipples luxuriously along the full length of his body from the groin upwards, till they are lying chest to chest, nipple to nipple, and mouth to mouth — and now the poet tastes the unsettling savour of his own male sex for the first time, on Elia's lips. He tries to speak to her, tries to laugh, though speech and laughter are almost impossible amid the intense, delightful waves of desire which are almost drowning him, choking his words and making him tremble from head to foot. Elia has to guess at his words, and his laugh sounds like a croak. "You've *got* the point of support!" he gasps. "Between the two of us we *can* move the world!" Then he slides into her, with a gasp of pure astonishment, because he still can't understand this miracle, even after experiencing it quite a number of times; he can't understand how that hidden, secret nest can be so warm and soft, as if upholstered in velvet, covered with the finest down; he

106

can't explain the infinitely tender feelings, so comforting that it brings tears to his eyes, that he has when he slides in very slowly, and the pleasure mounts up and up, and a fiery pang shoots up his back, and he thrusts and withdraws in unending succession, while she withdraws and returns again and again, pressing forward to meet his every movement, the all-embracing protectress, the creatress of a world in which there is no place for death. (Death and pleasure are one and the same; but, by a strange parodox, death ceases to exist when pleasure reaches its height — or perhaps we cannot see it because it is too close to us, as we float in the open sea of pleasure.) And then something happens inside Elia which is a clear sign that the end is not far away: he feels that most intimate of caresses, that slight, growing pressure, which seems to fold over on itself and cling to him like a ring of blood or fire. The first time this happened, the pressure was so slight that he hardly noticed it, and he didn't understand what it meant until several days later. "Why are you trying to push me out?" he asked finally, and she laughed and said "I'm *not* trying to push you out, silly!" She showed him what it meant and he finally understood, and he followed her into the most recondite of physical dialogues, skin to skin, until they both lost their footing amid the rushing waters of this river, amid the red sands of this stormy beach, and for a few seconds everything hung in suspense, and what was happening seemed impossible, unthinkable (his mother couldn't imagine it in a hundred years, thinks Ricardo, with a strange mixture of grief, anger and nostalgia). It seems inconceivable that vertigo itself can be a pleasure of this intensity, that the whole world can be centred on a few inches of skin, on a lever and a point of support which can indeed move the earth. Then Elia gasps, and her body goes limp on top of him, overlappng him on both sides and yet strangely weightless, with her arms and legs pointing in all directions

107

as if indicating the bearings of the four points of the compass from the very central point of the universe. Ricardo has a confused memory of a well-known drawing by Leonardo, that central point where the lever has again found its secret point of firm support, where the secret rite has again been fulfilled. Elia lets her head settle inertly into the hollow of Ricardo's shoulder, with rumpled hair, burning cheeks, lips twisted as if in pain, and eyes half-closed. He is strangely moved to feel the rhythm of her rapid, deep breathing. Presently Elia opens her eyes, and shifts her head off his shoulder and on to the pillow, making a vain attempt to get a better view of his face without losing contact at the centre.

Clara's mother was scolding her again: "Whatever has got into you now, to make you laugh at nothing all the time by yourself, like a lunatic?" Clara jumped and was uneasy for a few moments, as if she had been caught in the act, as if her greatest secret had suddenly been made public, as if there were really a risk of being understood by her mother or the others who went around being alarmed or suspicious or surprised about Clara, and asking her what she was laughing at. It wasn't really a laugh at all; it had a silent, inward, supremely happy quality which made it much more like a smile; but they still called it a laugh. And what risk could there be of their understanding it, or guessing what it meant, when they couldn't even tell a smile from a laugh? And yet it was obvious enough, really, because that smile was absolutely unique, quite different from all the smiles that might have existed in the past; it had only existed for a very short time. Clara reflected that if people would stop suspecting and being surprised and asking questions for a few moments and just opened their eyes and *looked*, they couldn't help knowing the answer, because it was obvious that her smile was a smile of love, and of the tenderness and pain of love, and that it couldn't be anything else. It was smile intended for one person and one person alone; it had never existed for anyone else in the past nor could it exist for anyone else in the future. It was the smile Clara smiles when she thinks of Elia. And she thinks of her all the time, she can't think about anything else, she can't concentrate on her reading or her work, she can't take in what other people say to her; her thoughts are so intensely fixed on Elia that it hurts her and drains her strength away. She goes to sleep thinking of Elia, dreams about her, and wakes up with an agony of deprivation, which she identifies a moment later as the agony of loving Elia so much and not being loved in return. On the edge of despair, on the brink of tears, Clara finds herself entertaining the blasphemous wish that she could stop thinking about Elia for a few minutes, just a few minutes rest and relief . . . Clara smiles that special smile when she remembers some trivial gesture of Elia's — the way she leans her golden head against the back of her rocking-chair, or the way she half closes her eyes to look at you; and then there's the way she sometimes covers her mouth with her hand, and Clara can't tell whether she's hiding a smile or hiding a yawn, can't be sure whether she is amusing Elia or boring her to death with the long stories she tells her — stories she has never told anyone before, and probably never will tell anyone again, although she can't tell whether they interest Elia or bore her. Elia encourages her to talk, forces her to talk in fact, and often seems to listen with great attention; but then she'll suddenly interrupt Clara (in the middle of an explanation that she's just asked her for), and start talking about something completely trivial and irrelevant, or get up to put a record on the gramophone or to water the flowers. And so Clara is left in the middle of a sentence, upset and embarrassed, and silently swearing that she'll never, never tell Elia anything

109

again . . . And Clara remembers the way Elia sits down with her feet tucked under her, on the sofa or the bed or the carpet, with a coca-cola in her hand, looking like a good little schoolgirl who has done her homework, to discuss the most improbable and outrageous theories.

And then another of Elia's gestures comes to Clara's mind. When Elia is ready to go to sleep, she thinks or pretends to think that Clara is ready too. The fact is that Clara, who can't swallow any food while Elia is there, also can't sleep when she's in bed with Elia, because the pleasure of proximity is too intense, and the opportunity of spending the night with Elia is too rare and precious. It has happened four times so far, but there's no knowing if it will ever happen again, and it is quite possible that Elia is aware of all this. Anyway, the time comes when Elia feels drowsy and consequently decides that it is time for both of them to go to sleep, and this is what she does. She smooths back Clara's hair, gives her a light kiss on the forehead, and carefully tucks the bedclothes around her; after which she turns her back and clasps the pillow in her arms. During every one of the four nights they have spent together, Elia has never gone to sleep with her arms round Clara, but always around the pillow; while Clara lies behind her, trembling with nervous strain and with fear at the thought that she might wake Elia up.

Clara remembers how Elia says goodbye to her at the door of the flat, with a smile that has something about it slightly uncomfortable, perhaps even faintly guilty; because there's always a feeling in the air that Clara is being driven out, even on occasions when she has got to go for reasons of her own. And so Elia smiles at her with sudden shyness and gently says "We'll see each other soon," or "We'll see each other tomorrow." Clara gropes her way blindly into the lift, across the hall and out of the door; she wanders aimlessly through the streets, and on some days she is overwhelmed with the happiness of loving and the joy of Elia's presence; for Elia's absence doesn't catch up with her immediately. It doesn't begin from the moment when Elia closes the door behind her, shutting it gently, as if she were afraid of hurting it; nor while Clara stumbles into the lift, so dazed that sooner or later she's bound to bump her nose against the frame of the door or against the banisters — how Elia would laugh if she could see her! "God, you are clumsy!" she'd say — and it may be several minutes before her absence catches up with you, several hours in fact; and in that case there is an interval of dreamy exaltation during which Clara can wander through the streets free from tension and sorrow, fulfilled and happy as she has never been in Elia's company. Perhaps love, as Clara understands it, always turns to happiness when it reaches its highest point; and in that case the best thing for her will be not to stop loving Elia, but to love her more and more, exceeding all the limits, passing the point of no return, loving her so much that love becomes sufficient unto itself, and it doesn't matter what Elia feels or ceases to feel, or what Elia still has to give — and in fact she probably feels nothing and has nothing further to offer. The thing is to love her beyond the bounds of hope . . . Some afternoons, when Clara leaves Elia's flat, she wanders for hours and hours through the streets, unhearing and unseeing, blundering through the crowds, in danger of getting run over, and always with that childish, sleepwalker's smile on her face. Strange to say, Clara has never smiled like that in Elia's presence. This is a smile which Elia has never seen, because it is indissolubly linked with her absence. Elia will never see that sensitive, tender smile, with its touch of sadness; and yet it springs from love for her, and no one else will ever be able to call it forth.

Another equally curious thing is this: Clara is normally rather a silent person, but Elia has persuaded and stimulated her into breaking her silence, so that now she talks a lot and tells Elia about very secret and private matters; and yet the passionate, interminable monologue that fills Clara's mind when she is alone forms no part of what she says to Elia when they meet — or even when they part . . . When they are face to face, or body to body, Clara never utters the tender, passionate, desolate words of adoration and supplication which run through her head as she walks through the streets, or lies in the darkness of her bedroom, staring at the ceiling or pressing her face against the pillow.

And then there's something Clara doesn't understand, though she's thought a lot about it and invented all sorts of practical-sounding reasons: there are days when Elia's moods — which vary from the affectionate and absent-minded to the irritable and even slightly aggressive — seem to cover up an underlying, unchanging substratum of remoteness and indifference. "Why ever does she ask me to come and see her?" wonders Clara on those unhappy days. "Why does she want me to be at her side? Why does she take me off to bed with her when I haven't asked for anything or said anything about it?" There has been nothing in Elia's behaviour and nothing has happened at any of their meetings, which could justify the alternation of ecstasy and despair in Clara's heart. Perhaps the feeling of desolation that comes over Clara some evenings is due to a faltering in her love for Elia, a fatigue caused by the strain of loving her in a vacuum, without return or hope. Perhaps it is the falling off of her own love which makes Elia's lack of love so intolerable. With these thoughts running in her head, Clara walks unsteadily out of Elia's flat, and is swallowed up in the street outside. It's even worse when this happens in the pitiless light of morning; she stumbles out with her mind blank and a confused but inexorable feeling in her heart that she has nothing more to give, that there's nothing more she can do, and yet she can't help going on, because there is no other way to go. Clara sways as she crosses the street, and steadies herself against the wall; with a great effort, she manages to stop a taxi and tell the driver where the wants to go. When she gets home, she pushes her brothers aside, makes some excuse to her mother, and shuts herself up in her bedroom. She puts out the light, and lies on the bed with her face to the wall, with a strange bitterness flooding her mouth and burning her throat. (Clara never knew till now that the bitterness of which poets tell us is a real, physical thing, a vile taste in the mouth which seems to have no end, because when you think you've swallowed it all and got rid of it, it's suddenly there again, and you have to begin again from the beginning.) Clara lies there contemplating a decision like someone contemplating a poisoned cup, trying to make up her mind never to see Elia again, not to answer the telephone, never to go back to that flat . . .

Even on the other days, the days of ecstasy, Clara's smile has something sad and fearful about it; for she is in fact terribly afraid. This is partly because of what Ricardo has been saying when he rings her up — which he is doing as incessantly as ever: "Elia is fed up with your gloom, your reproaches and your sulky face," he says; and "You bore her stiff with your clumsiness, can't you do better than that?;" and "You know quite well that what you do in bed doesn't mean a thing to her;" and "She's going to end up by hating you if you go on making her feel so infernally guilty." It is useless for Clara to implore him to stop. It is futile for her to threaten to tell Elia what he has been saying, because he knows all too well that she will never carry that threat out. But Ricardo's words are not the only thing which make Clara tremble with apprehension and fear. They are not the only thing that makes it impossible for her to be certain, even for a moment, that what is happening to her has any basis in

113

reality, and impossible for her even to hope that it may have a future, so that her love for Elia is poisoned by despair and fear, by the knowledge that she may lose her at any moment and by the unbearable thought that she may in fact never have had anything real to lose . . . But this is not all Ricardo's fault, though his shadow is always present between the two women — why does Elia allow this? wonders Clara, why does she love him so much? — and although he seems to be engaged in some strange manoeuvres, which Clara does not fully understand but which she finds alarming. A memory which is also a premonition stirs in Clara's mind — Ricardo's story about one of his classmates and how they used to caress each other under cover of their desk during the metrical composition lesson. Although Ricardo always uses the word love when telling the story, it isn't really love at all. Ricardo didn't love his desk-mate, and he doesn't really love Elia either. (The very fact of having entertained this thought, of having put it in words even to herself, fills Clara with guilt.) No, it's something else — Ricardo's deskmate was selected in cold blood, and the same is true of Elia. There were several good reasons for Ricardo's earlier choice; his companion was the best looking and strongest boy in the class, he came of the best family, and he had the most open and engaging cha- racter of any of them. After careful calculation, Ricardo had chosen him and had at once embarked on a patient, obstinate pursuit of his quarry. With a superb display of intelligence, or perhaps merely of cunning, pretending to feel every shade of tenderness and passion, planning each move like a champion chess player, and all this not because he really loved the other boy, but because he needed him to prove something to the world, or, more significantly, to himself. It was essential for Ricardo to subjugate his partner, and drag him into his own playing-field. It was essential that his words should be law. And he must be free to tell everyone about it

114

— a stipulation which he made later with Elia. Clara reflects that it may not have been chance, not a simple case of bad luck, that the two boys were discovered with their trousers undone and their hands busy under the desk. If it was Ricardo who gave them away, it was probably not an accident. The other boy took on the significance of a symbol or myth, a pretext cunningly calculated to mask something else. Ricardo had set him up as a symbol in order to score a victory over all the others. And it was in the same spirit that he had subsequently selected Elia, falling in love with her or thinking he had fallen in love with her before he really knew her, so that you could see that she too had been transformed into a myth and an emblem. He had selected her rather than another woman because of her social position, her prestige, her charm and her intelligence, and not really out of love at all.

Clara can imagine Ricardo's reply to that:

"Yes, I do love her for all those reasons; and how about you? Why do you love her? You could have fallen in love with any of your university friends, or any of your mother's friends, or one of your neighbours; but you chose Elia because she is prettier, more quick-witted, more gifted and more elegant. You love her for what she represents and for what surrounds her just as much as I do."

That's what Ricardo would say, with a triumphant laugh; but it wasn't true, Clara didn't love Elia because of all that. Love wasn't a total you got by adding all those things up — not for Clara, at least, even if it did seem to be true for Ricardo. For Clara, love meant something quite different. Ricardo had probably chosen Elia after a careful calculation based on the necessity of proving various things to himself and to other people. In the same way, he had needed at an earlier stage to prove that even the clumsiest and least attractive boy at school, even the worst at games, even the

115

least popular with the other boys — unpopular with the masters, too, although he was always head of the class — could make use of love, or something he regarded as love, to establish complete dominion over the strongest, best looking and best liked of his companions. And that was why that episode was so important to Ricardo, who had told the whole story to Clara, though he'd certainly told Elia only half of it. It wasn't a story of love, but a story of a solitary struggle against the world, in which the other boy had merely been made use of; and that was why the end of the story was so painful — the final chapter which he probably hadn't mentioned to Elia, though he had told Clara all about it.

The worst of it, said Ricardo, was not when they were caught with their trousers down and their hands busy under the desk, nor when their parents were told about it and went into exaggerated demonstrations of disgust and horror, nor when he and his friend were kept isolated from each other and their companions for hours every day, praying in the chapel, nor when they were subjected to interminable and ridiculous interrogations, threats and exorcisms; all that was not too unbearable, he said (and Clara, suspected that it might even have been to some extent programmed); it had simply been even more stupid than he expected. And then he pretended to give in and repent, to undergo an ostentatious and theatrical conversion for the edification of all and sundry, so that he scored a double victory over his astonished schoolmates, who had been defeated twice, once in the fields of vice and once in the fields of virtue, by the clumsy swot who had always been the ugly duckling of his class, and indeed of the whole school. He had been isolated from his first day at school because he was different from the others, isolated (in his own view, and to some extent in Clara's) because the others detected in him an intelligence and a sensibility which they did not fully understand but instinc-

116

tively felt to be a threat; and these were in fact the very qualities with which he had (or sometimes thought he had) got the better of his schoolmates, his masters and his family . . .

And so Ricardo had become the holiest of the holy, the purest of the pure; but then something happened which he could never have imagined. From time to time he met his old desk-mate in the corridors or at the door of the chapel, and always greeted him with a humourous, conspiritorial wink or an affectionate, mocking grimace, never thinking that the other boy might be genuinely frightened and sincerely repentant, that he would really give in and let Ricardo down. Ricardo was amazed by what happened a few weeks later, when their punishment came to an end. They knelt for the last time to take Communion at the special rail to the right of the altar; and after the service they were sent back to their class and to their normal studies. (They had initially been threatened with explusion, but this had been abandoned in view of the convincing nature of their repentance. But when Ricardo smilingly laid his hand on the other boy's trousers, with an air of symbolical renewal, his friend stopped him, and said, with a sad and frightened look, and with real sincerity in his eyes: "Leave me alone . . . that's a sin, and now I've repented and never want to do it again." And so all Ricardo's patient, persistent work, his cautious, intelligent propaganda in favour of vice and pleasure, the whole spider's web into which he had woven the threads of power and control over the other boy, were tangled and broken at a stroke; and Ricardo himself was condemned by the stupidity of his partner, by his unheard of, inconceivable feebleness of spirit, to start again from scratch — perhaps on a foundation provided by Clara, perhaps on one provided years later by Elia — and to rebuild his complex, artificial edifice of self-esteem — or perhaps a more modest castle of self-confidence.

117

Clara wonders why they asked her to come round today; and why Elia sounded so odd on the telephone. It was like a stranger's voice, artificial, metallic and uneasy — quite unlike her usual grave and beautiful tones. Clara sometimes thinks that it was hearing Elia's voice that first made her fall in love with her, though plenty of other good reasons followed immediately afterwards . . . And why has Elia asked both of them to come round at the same time; — assuming, that is, that Ricardo has been invited and hasn't just decided to pay Elia a visit because of some chance whim or in keeping with one of his long calculated plans. Anyway, here they are, in this flat which is the secret heaven of the cats, and which has come very close to providing Clara with a real home. Today, however, Ricardo is there, and the flat seems like a different place. The three of them have never met here before; they've sometimes met in cafés, but never all three of them together in the flat. There's suddenly something threatening about this protective retreat, as if your worst enemy might be hidden somewhere inside it. Clara had thought she'd found a secret refuge there, where she could be safe and recover from her wounds, comforted by Elia's velvety voice, by the huge windows wide open to the sunshine and the song of the birds, by the great rooms with their soft carpets and hangings; and now it's a painful shock to realise that this very refuge may have been penetrated by the worst of all dangers, the cruellest and most insidious of enemies. When this happens, the hunted animal — myself, for instance, thinks Clara — doesn't know whether to go on deeper into its refuge in search of some better protected nook, or to turn round and bolt for the open country . . . Elia seems quite different today, too; she moves around as if she weren't on her own territory, and she won't even let Clara make the tea, as she always does, but goes into the kitchen herself (which is something Clara has never seen her do before). She heats the water and

118

ill-temperedly dumps tea-bags into the cups, like they do in cafés. She doesn't seem to care any more about the proper way of making tea; nothing seems to matter very much to Elia today. She is very silent and abstracted, with an expression on her face that's quite different from the look of depressive boredom or angry impatience that Clara knows so well. This is an expression of utter indifference and withdrawal. It seems that Elia wants to reduce her participation in what is going on to a minimum; or perhaps, thinks Clara with a shudder, she wants to keep right out of what might follow. Presently Ricardo rolls some reefers, and all three of them light up; but Elia's abstracted, evasive manner remains unchanged, and she hardly puts the cigarette to her lips — which doesn't surprise Clara, because she knows that Elia doesn't like hashish or marijuana. Ricardo doesn't even notice that Elia isn't smoking; his sole concern seems to be that Clara should inhale correctly and let the smoke out slowly. He is very insistent about this, and Clara looks appealing to Elia for advice, for some indication of what she should do. Finally Elia interrupts her sulky, withdrawn, abstracted reverie for long enough to indicate that Clara should do what Ricardo says, and try to smoke her reefer properly. So Clara breathes in deeply, inhaling the smoke, which seems to scorch and burn her throat and lungs, keeps it in as long as she can, and breathes it out very slowly, conscious as she does so that she must look very like a conscientious, obedient little girl trying not to disappoint her mother . . . Clara began to feel slightly sick, not altogether because of the drug, but rather because of an indefinable feeling of apprehension — a secret terror of the wild beast which has not yet made its appearance, though she can smell it and knows it is there, in the innermost recesses of the cave which is her refuge; for this fearsome beast doesn't run down its prey in the open, but lies in wait in the depths of the cave.

119

It is all the more terrifying because it hasn't yet declared itself, and she doesn't know what it looks like or what it is. There's just a vague smell of animals and of danger which alarms and disgusts her. Then she reflects that there can't really be any cause for fear while she is in the cats' heaven, with Elia at her side. For a moment Clara feels that her recent doubts, fears and distress have been an act of treason towards Elia, into whose hands she has entrusted her life and her very being. It is inconceivable to Clara that there can be any other kind of love but this, any love without the abnegation expressed in the words "Be it done unto me according to thy word", any love subject to manipulation or bargaining, or a love where the lover gives only half of himself. Such is Clara's creed; although Ricardo thinks she is crazy and calls her a fool, and even Elia has sometimes laughed at her and warned her against it: "You can't love like that," she says, "you ought not to love me so much." Even Elia has advised Clara to keep a card up her sleeve, as if the possibility of cheating were the whole point of the game. But Clara doesn't cheat, and doesn't regard love as a game . . . For Clara, love means total surrender of the self, which must include perfect trust; so what room is there for apprehension or fear? And yet they are still there, while she goes on diligently smoking, scorching her throat and choking as she does so because Elia told her to — though did she say it in words, or did she just move her hand in an ambiguous and scarcely perceptible gesture? They are still there as she drinks several glasses of champagne, which Ricardo pours out for her, apparently just as intent on filling her glass and seeing her empty it as he was previously on seeing her inhale deeply and breathe out slowly. What a funny idea to open up a bottle of French champagne just after they'd been drinking tea, especially as neither Elia nor Clara like it. Clara drinks the champagne, because Elia has told her to, although she isn't thirsty and

120

doesn't like it, although she is beginning to feel really queasy and knows it won't agree with her. And in spite of logic and reason, in spite of love and loyalty, that secret fear goes on growing in her heart, that silent apprehension takes on a more solid form; the terrifying beast is watching them from the back of the cave, invisible but betrayed by its smell. Clara feels the need of Dutch courage; she begins to drink and smoke of her own accord, without any prompting or encouragement from the others. She does this not only to please Elia, who doesn't even look at her and has avoided meeting her eyes ever since she arrived at the flat, nor to avoid annoying Ricardo, who never takes his eyes off her for a moment. She is now smoking and drinking in a desperate attempt to deaden her feelings, her thoughts and her fears, so that she can reach the climax of the coming nightmare in a partially anaesthetised condition.

And now it is clear that the nightmare is a real nightmare, in which all Clara's apprehensions and fears are justified; and it seems that its climax is going to take place in Elia's bedroom, with its pink velvet hangings and its pink carpet, with its gilt-framed mirrors and its mirrors framed in ebony, with its paintings and drawings of naked women, asleep or half-asleep, lying down or sitting up, indifferent or expectant, alone or surrounded by real or legendary animals. And there are other pictures too: pictures of some devoted lover of Elia's, of gentlemen in tail-coats and top-hats, and coloured photographs of the two children. This is the same bedroom where Clara has so often seen the Queen of the Cats dozing, and so often seen her bored or depressed; it is the room where Clara has so often sat at Elia's side as she lay hidden beneath the blankets or stretched out on top of the great bed . . . it has a cream-coloured chenille coverlet on it today, which Clara hasn't seen before. And now Elia takes off the coverlet, pushing Muslina absent-mindedly aside with a rough

121

movement that isn't like her at all, with such mechanical indifference that Clara feels personally offended and humiliated, in total sympathy with the cat. Muslina stalks away in a dignified manner, with upright tail and hair standing up along her spine; in her eyes is that cold, disdainful look (more remote even than Elia's) which cats use to hide their wrath. Cats seem to compress their anger into a sort of icicle, thinks Clara. It freezes and burns at the same time, like that special ice you used to find sometimes on the outside of tubs or bars of ice cream when you were small, a sort of magic ice which burned your fingers and bubbled and smoked if you dropped it into a glass . . . Anyway, Elia has taken the coverlet off the bed and is folding it up with great care, taking no notice of Muslina's disgust. On other occasions, the coverlet has been bundled together anyhow and thrown on the pink carpet at the foot of the bed; but today Elia is so absorbed in the task of folding it that you'd think she had nothing else in the world to do but shape it into a perfectly symmetrical package, while Ricardo undresses Clara, who remains quite passive and does not resist. As he takes off her clothes, he says the most grotesque and terrible things to her, things which are meant to sound passionate but which make her want to die of shame and terror, though they are supremely ridiculous as well. She wonders where he got them from, from which of the squalid little books he hides so carefully from his virtuous mother, this skinny, awkward boy, with long, greasy hair sticking to the back of his neck, with dull eyes and with spots all over his cheeks and temples . . . And now that he's taken off his own clothes, Clara can see that he has more purplish spots on his chest, back and shoulders, this angry-looking adolescent, with his sweaty hands and viscous saliva; Ricardo has just pressed his mouth against her mouth, and is sucking with his lips and pushing with his tongue — and Clara realises with utter dismay that

122

the anaesthetic isn't going to work, that she's got to live through what's coming to her in a state of complete consciousness. The effects of the hemp and the alcohol have been dissipated in a couple of moments, swept away by Ricardo's touch, Ricardo's words and gestures, and Ricardo's smell, which must surely be the smell of the beast that was lying in wait for her at the back of the cave. All that's left is a persistent feeling of nausea, and she can't be sick here, not over the linen sheets, the chenille coverlet or the pink carpet. She isn't going to cry, either, not in front of Ricardo, or the remote, sleep-walking, treacherous Queen of the Cats, although Clara's eyelids are burning. She knows that the mad fire which shines from Ricardo's eyes, the sweatiness of his hands, the irregularity of his breathing, and the eagerness with which he kisses her and hugs her and nibbles and sucks at her has nothing to do with love, and very little to do with desire. It's something quite different — a complicated game in which he tries to score off the devil, his fellows, or perhaps even himself; a game which he began to play long ago, probably even before he won the heart of his desk-companion during the metrical composition class. Everything about it is false — the frenzy, the ecstasy, the love, and even the sex. And Clara says as much to Elia, who has finally finished chivvying cats and folding coverlets and has taken off her clothes and got into bed with the other two, displacing Ricardo and taking Clara in her arms. The boy is left lying behind Elia, temporarily exiled to the edge of the magic circle woven by the embraces of the two women, who are lying belly to belly, with their legs interlocked and their heads very close together on the pillow. Clara whispers to Elia in the thick tones of a drunken woman; perhaps the marijuana or the champagne have had some effect after all. "That boy," she says, "is just playing chess with the devil!" Elia is surprised for a moment, and then pleased and comforted to see that

123

Clara is making a joke, that she's capable of ordinary conversation. Elia begins to think that what is happening may have no serious consequences, that Ricardo may be right about it. Elia seems much happier and more at ease; she laughs and finally looks Clara straight in the eyes. "Yes," she says conspiratorially, "they want to establish which of them will come off best, pitting intelligence against intelligence and power against power." Clara nods gravely, almost overcome by the terrible, agonising physical temptation to burst into tears, to collapse sobbing into Elia's arms (especially now that Elia is talking to her in her normal voice and looking her straight in the eyes and even smiling at her) and loudly demand that she should send Ricardo away at once, that she should get rid of this ugly, devious, dirty young man, whose presence has already soiled the heaven of the cats, the bedroom of the feline sleeping beauty, the bed of the Queen of the Cats; and then the two of them could stay alone together for the rest of the evening, as they often had before; and it's quite possible that if he goes now everything can still be put right. . . . But Clara nods gravely and says nothing of all this, probably because if she started to talk she'd burst into tears, and it's difficult enough to avoid doing that anyway. Elia smiles a relieved smile and puts her arm round Clara's shoulders; with her other hands she strokes her cheek and smooths the hair back away from her eyes; then she kisses her on the ears, on the neck and on the lips. Finally Clara speaks again; she wants to say "Get rid of him! It's not too late. Send him away!", but she chokes the words back. In a voice so low that she seems to be talking to herself — the voice of a little girl trying not to cry — she says: "But neither of them know anything about love." Elia must have heard her, although she spoke in the faintest of whispers, because she stops kissing her and looks at her sadly, with a nervous laugh. "No, no, Clara," she says, "you're quite right about

124

that. There are three of us in the same boat — the devil, Ricardo and myself, and none of us knows anything about love." And now the two women shut their eyes, and their kisses grow warmer, deeper and more prolonged; they caress each other's cheeks, shoulders and breasts — but then Clara's attention is brutally distracted, divided in two in fact, as she feels Ricardo's naked body come into contact with her back, pressing itself tightly against her. She feels his hard, damp hands running over her sides and buttocks, and she feels them slide up to her breasts, pushing Elia's soft, delicate hands aside. She feels the roughness of his tongue, the sucking of his hot lips, the soiling contact of his thick saliva on the back of her neck, all down her back, and between her legs. Then she feels his organ pressing against her; and she is swept again by waves of almost uncontrollable nausea, and feels herself on the point of bursting into tears and completely losing control of herself. She can feel rough hands pulling her thighs apart and hurting her as they search for a refuge, a nest for that dreadful object . . . how *can* Elia thinks of it as a bird? wonders Clara. She struggles and wriggles and tries to resist, although she is too drunk, or too doped, or perhaps simply too depressed to put up much of a fight; and Elia is there, too, still stroking and caressing her . . . If only she could forget that other terrible presence behind her! Elia rocks her and cradles her and cuddles and holds her in position. It's as if I were a timid young mare and didn't want to be mounted by the stallion they'd chosen for me, thinks Clara bitterly. Elia goes on kissing her, and murmurs gently between kisses: "Keep still, my love, he isn't going to hurt you; keep still, my pretty kitten, my little girl, my beauty."

Ricardo heard Elia's voice say "the devil, Ricardo and I are all in the same boat; none of us know anything about love," although he did not know that she was repeating what Clara had said before, because Clara was on the far side of Elia and had spoken in a whisper, as she so often did. He found both their voices intensely annoying. Clara's soft, hesitant tones reminded him of the insipid whining of a frightened little girl; and Clara was not a litle girl any more, nor did she have any reason to be frightened or distressed. Even more annoying were Elia's affected words, obviously spoken for him to hear. Just third class literature, like dialogue out of a book by Françoise Sagan (whose works Elia actually *likes*) or from some film of the *nouvelle vague*. "The devil, Ricardo and I are all in the same boat," she says, "none of us know anything about love!" And now her empty, pedantic words have ruined this exquisite interior, with its pink carpet and velvet, its mirrors and pictures and porcelain, and the three of them naked in the huge bed, the two women and himself, and everything in its place, everything in exactly the place previously planned and chosen for it. Ricardo had in fact been planning this for a long time — since the very first day that he visited Elia's flat, and she took him into her bedroom to show him some photographs of the children which she could not find in the cupboard or the chest of drawers, which were full to bursting with clothes; silks, cambrics, lace and ribbons poured out of the drawers like cascades of white or pink foam. It was at that early stage, when Ricardo was weaving the main threads of this complex story, that he foresaw that the turning point would take place here, and not in one of the crazy bedrooms of the houses of assignation. They were fine for his previous meetings with Elia, but no good for Clara, no good for the threesome act they had to perform with Clara. (There's no place for the devil in all this; why bring him into it?) The turning-point had to be here, on a Sunday afternoon, with the sun coming obliquely through the cracks of the shutters, and the song of the cage-birds and the

wild birds outside in the trees. That Sunday afternoon would
be fulfilment or culmination of a long series of other Sunday
afternoons, which could then be forgotten — afternoons he
had spent alone in his bedroom, listening to his mother's
steps in the passage outside. Prying was her speciality, not
companionship, so he was all alone with his books and his
papers, imagining crazy, orgiastic scenes in which the lead-
ing parts were at first generally played by faceless women and
faceless boys; though on rare occasions he visualised the boys
with the features of his desk companion in the metrical
composition class, or a woman with the features of some
well-known film actress or an illustration from some
pornographic novelette. Later on, a girl with Clara's face
came into his daydreams, and later still a nymph-like woman
with Elia's features. Last of all, just a few weeks ago, Elia and
Clara appeared together in his visions, which began to take
on the form of threesomes of infinite variety and
seductiveness. (Figures of other women or boys would
sometimes appear on the outskirts of the group — but not the
devil! never the devil! What an idea to bring him into it!) So
alluring were those threefold visions that it had been quite
easy to impose them on Elia, who could never resist any
temptation that might offer a few hours escape from her
terrible disgust with her own image; for she is still terrified of
mirrors, although in fact her greatest attraction lies in her
satiny, fragrant beauty, and in the splendour of the exquisite
décors amid which she passes her empty existence. Ricardo
finds it extraordinary that Clara, who has so obstinately and
unreasonably refused to love him, has nevertheless been able
to evolve the tenderest and most touching of images for Elia,
turning her into the Little Queen of the Cats, when really she
is nothing but an attractive, bored, rich woman, not even
terribly intelligent; certainly not as intelligent as himself or
Clara, nor all that interesting . . . Anyway, here the three of

127

them are in the pink bedroom, with sunshine and birdsong filtering through the shutters — and no cats. That's in deference to my wishes, thinks Ricardo. Pets inspire him with nothing but repulsion or fear, and he hates them all; he feels sick at the thought that a few minutes ago Muslina was lying exactly where he is now . . . Yes, this Sunday afternoon is the culmination and redemption of all those other afternoons. Here is Elia, a rich and attractive woman, with a good deal of childish naughtiness about her, not really very intelligent, though one must admit that she's bright and inventive and witty. Passionately bored with life, she tries to convert her boredom into the centre of the universe, if you let her get away with it; she tries to use it as the intellectual foundation for a lot of cunning, improbable, symmetrically constructed episodes, or to personify it as the chief master of ceremonies, the skilful puppet-master making his marionettes dance in front of a paper backdrop . . . And here is Clara, a girl in love, who is just that and nothing more, a stock character, a stereotype, typical to the point of being impersonal — a girl who loves with total, unreasoning, unending and unde-manding abnegation, although she would not and apparently cannot love him . . . Anyway, the last traces of common-sense, the last vestiges of the critical spirit, seem to be lost beyond recall; Clara has burnt her boats, lowered her drawbridge, pulled down her battlements, and destroyed the walls of her fortress from within. "Be it done unto me according to thy word" is certainly her motto — and what a monotonous, boring affair that sort of love must be for poor Elia, who has no idea where to put it or what to do with it! The only word that counts for anything at the moment is Ricardo's word; there is no significance left in anything either of the two women has to say, as Ricardo lies naked on the bed with the two female bodies, stretched out against Clara's back . . . And now he crosses over Clara's body, as you might

128

cross the rampart of a castle or a hedge covered with pale roses, like the white roses you always see on altars and coffins, and places himself between the two women, separating them like a man cutting a peach into two equal and symmetrical halves. First he kisses Elia's smooth, juicy mouth, with its greedy lips hungrily opening and coming forward to meet him, waiting for him already opened, flooded with saliva, redolent of honey; and her tongue springs silently forward, swift and astonishing as a snake emerging from among the flowers, shooting down the throat of her lover. Then Ricardo's lips seek that other mouth, with its slightly rough lips — Clara's mouth is always a little chapped by the cold or the wind. Her lips are tightly shut like those of an obstinate schoolgirl who has been unjustly scolded in class, who has been punished by loss of playtime or pudding, and she keeps her mouth tight shut for fear of letting a moan or a sob escape, or perhaps out of pure pigheadedness. Next Ricardo kisses Elia's shoulders and cheeks and throat, which are silky, golden brown and freckled, all smoothly and equally tanned by the sun of early summer to that beautiful colour which can only be acquired by lazy, spoilt women who can sunbathe on a private terrace, amid potted gardenias and the song of caged canaries. He imagines Elia lying there with her eyes shut, one hand holding a book and the other mechanically stroking her cat. Elia's skin is luxurious and aromatic, impregnated with oils smelling of coconut and honeysuckle; her shoulders and the back of her neck are perfect, with their silky touch and their warm exciting smell of the adult female. Then Ricardo kisses the dry skin of Clara's shoulders, and the back of her neck, which is covered with a short down like the down of a bird — and Clara is really trembling like a bird trembles when you hold it gently in your hand. Her skin is very white and vulnerable, subject to sudden spasms of trembling or twitching, caused by some senseless fear or

incomprehensible repugnance; they run across her skin as
lightning runs across a milky sky before a storm. Her sharp,
angular bones threaten to pierce her skin at certain points,
and there is a sour, pathetic smell of recent sweat about her,
like a terrified little animal — not like a bird, this time,
because birds don't sweat when you hold them in your hand,
but just tremble in feeble terror, with their beaks open. At
this point Ricardo is surprised to find himself thinking about
his mother; there is in fact something about Clara's pale,
angular, vulnerable and unalluring body which reminds him
of his mother. When he looks at Elia, on the other hand, every
trace of that maternal image is swallowed up and cancelled in
the golden and velvety, perfumed and peach-like skin, in the
hungry yet satisfied flesh of the adult woman. Ricardo runs
his finger tips over Elia's round and fragrant breasts, which
end in small, rosy nipples that seem to call out to him; they
look like the breasts of a youthful naiad lying peacefully on
her back amid the waters. Next he runs his fingers over
Clara's little breasts, with their unexpectedly wrinkled,
rough and dark-coloured nipples, which seem absolutely out
of place in this almost sexless body, like that of a slim little
girl; they are surprising, exciting, and somehow touching,
like the ugly marks left on her ribs, shoulders and back by the
straps of her brassiere, which have left deep grooves in her
delicate skin. Clara evidently squeezes her childish breasts,
which can hardly be said to exist apart from their large,
violet-coloured nipples, into a tight, stiff, ugly brassiere like
those worn by Ricardo's mother — utterly unlike the scanty
covering of cream-coloured silk, luxurious and decorative,
which sometimes encloses Elia's golden breasts. Ricardo puts
his cheek on Elia's bosom, lays his hands flat on her body,
and begins to run his lips and tongue over her smooth belly.
Then he does the same to Clara, who has a thin line of dark
hair running down from her navel, between her projecting

130

hipbones, which really look as if they might pierce through the skin at any moment, towards the hidden recess between her thighs; rather like an arrow pointing the way, thinks Ricardo, but he does not say so out loud, but merely smiles silently to himself, because he knows that Clara would not be amused by this thought. He slides his hands up to the waist and then to the breasts, first of one woman and then of the other; he caresses their breasts and shoulders again, and then he presses his lips into that warm nook between the thighs. Elia's is moist and fragrant as a ripe fruit (perhaps a fruit on the verge of being overripe); Clara's bristles with a hostile mass of black hair. Clara is keeping her legs pressed together with savage obstinacy, so that Ricardo has to slide his hands into position and push her thighs apart, while she struggles and cries out. It sounds like the cry of sea-birds ringing from cliff to cliff. Presently it seems to the poet that Elia is protesting too, although he's not listening much and doesn't take in what she is saying as he slides up alongside Clara's stimulatingly rigid body, carrying the taste of her sex on his lips, so that he can pass it to her from mouth to mouth, like a mouthful of cigarette smoke or champagne. Better than anything else he likes that exchange of the taste and aroma of sex, that flavour of lovely ripe fruit on the verge of being overripe, that perfume which recalls the depths of the ocean, and, above all, that discovery of his own secret savour on the lips of his partner in love; though Clara has obstinately refused to love him. So Ricardo slides up alongside the thin, awkward, vulnerable body, which has now begun to twist and struggle violently. The storm predicted by those flashes of lightning in the milky summer sky now seems to have broken up, and Clara is weeping loudly, like a little girl who has been unfairly punished in class and who has held back her tears for a very long time, so that the final outburst of weeping is so terrible and so violent that you'd think it was going to drown

131

the world. Clara weeps and screams and struggles, jerking her head from side to side on the pillow to avoid the touch of his lips, writhing away from him, hitting him, trying to push him away; while he grips her legs tightly between his knees, as if riding a half-broken filly, and goes on obstinately trying to find her mouth with his lips. Suddenly he finds that it is Elia who is hitting him, pulling him off Clara and moving her away from him to the edge of the bed. "Can't you see she doesn't like it?" she says. "Give her a chance! Leave her alone." Ricardo feels himself swamped by the impotent frustration and rage that have plagued him for years, multiplied a thousandfold and condensed into this moment. All his ancient anger is now concentrated on these two women, so stupid and yet so beautiful. Why, he wonders, do women have to be so beautiful and so impossible, so absurd and irrational, so incapable of understanding, so unpredictable and arbitrary in their actions, so inferior in almost every respect, so far from being his equals and yet so thoroughly capable of sweeping him off his feet and swallowing him up like a whirlwind carrying all things, living and inanimate, up into the sky, so thoroughly capable of keeping him dependent on them, enslaved and crazy for them, capable above all of ensnaring him by means of the restless wild bird which leads its own throbbing, independent life between his thighs, taking its decisions and making its own choices, dragging him after it with all his faculties, including his logical, reasonable mind ... These women know how to make the whole world — the world of men — turn around them, with their arrows of delicate fur pointing deceitfully towards the nest that lies between their thighs, with the warm, soft, moist recess that grips each wandering, searching wild bird in a ring of down and a ring of fire, nests to be penetrated abruptly or slid into slowly like precious, unfathomable middens, full of the bitter, penetrating odour

132

of the female in heat; Ricardo remembers Elia saying something on that subject, about the great apes wandering uneasily and hungrily around the dens of their females, having scented them out over a distance of several miles, from the other end of the springtime jungle . . . Well, here they both are now. Here's the supposedly adult woman, who is bored with life, who has no other attraction apart from her physical beauty (which she does not seem to care about) and who isn't even capable of playing a game through to the end. The most charitable supposition, thinks Ricardo bitterly, is that she must be jealous. And here's this skinny, sweaty girl, who wastes so much time refusing him, with her obstinate, absurd whimsy of not loving him. And now on the other side of the bed, at the far end of the springtime jungle, where Elia has put her, she's sobbing and screaming as if she'd gone off her head or were terrified of something — terrified of what? he wonders. And now Elia, too, has gone stiff and is turning away and rejecting him, like a fleshy, sensitive orchid reacting to an alien touch. Ricardo grabs Elia by the shoulders and shakes her; it can't be true that she can be so stupid, that both of them can be so stupid, that they should treat him like this. He hits Elia several times in the face with the flat of his hand, and bites her neck and her mouth until he tastes or thinks he tastes the bitter-sweet taste of her blood. And suddenly Elia moans softly, and looks at him with huge, wide-opened eyes, astonished and terrified; then she sighs and purrs and begins to press her whole body against him. Her hand feels for him, excites him and guides him safely into harbour, into the secret nest; and Ricardo penetrates her with such strength, such lust and such rage, that this time he reaches the far end of the recess and batters brutally against it. Elia's eyes are very still and wide open; she does not moan or cry out, and the bedroom begins to rotate slowly in an ascending spiral. Ricardo wonders if the two of them are

133

being sucked up into one of those black whirlwinds which throng in the upper air and sometimes engulf him. They drift on and up in the blood-red spiral, amid scarlet bedclothes and hangings, the liquid fire of sunlight coming in through the windows, and the red flames of birdsong. Never before have Ricardo and Elia desired each other, sought and found each other with such savage zest; never again will love be like this for them, like this unique, unrepeatable experience, with both of them crazy with frustration, resentment and rage, their mutual hatred and contempt sharpened by the fact that their bodies irresistibly continue to desire and seek each other. In each ferocious assault, the desire to fulfil and possess is mingled with a craving to destroy and annihilate; he thrusts into her again and again as if he were stabbing her repeatedly with a dagger in the chest or the throat ... Perhaps this moistness is blood, and perhaps this smell is the smell of blood, this persistent odour of overripeness and of the sea, this bitter, delicious and intolerable perfume. He feels a vertigo mounting with the rhythm of the spiral rising towards the sky, the black, irrevocable whirlwind ... Someone seems to be screaming. Perhaps it's Clara, who must be watching them, thinks Ricardo, unable to take her eyes off them, however much she covers her face with her hands. Perhaps it's Elia, who is beside herself in the intoxication of desire, like a splendid angel of abundance and death. Or perhaps it's Ricardo himself, crying out without being aware of it. Suddenly, abruptly he turns Elia's body around. He's in sole command here now, and no other wishes or thoughts count for anything except those of the rutting male in the rutting jungle. He turns Elia around, roughly tugging and slapping her body, and makes her kneel on the sheet with her rump in the air and her face buried in the pillow. Then he mounts her and rides her as he imagines that the great apes mount and ride their females in the jungle,

134

from behind, so that the two partners can't look at each other, or kiss each other or speak to each other, each of them infinitely remote and solitary, without the faintest hope of communication or tenderness . . . This is a faceless Elia (he can only see her auburn hair spread over the pillow), a voiceless Elia, who has finally lost the power of speech and has no sweet kisses for him, no soft caresses for his cheeks, nothing but her magnificent haunches, firm and splendid as the curving wooden sides of a ship, the haunches of a female in rut, of a female in flower, embracing, absorbing haunches, rocked in a powerful swell that carries all before it; the compass is out of action, the rudder is broken and the sails are in shreds . . . Her waist is slim and shapely, movingly fragile in appearance; her back is a golden brown, with a slight furrow down the middle and just a hint of the delicate bony structure beneath; and finally her head vanishes into the pillow, beneath a sea of red and gold curls. The delicious, detestable Queen of the Cats has been reduced to a madly twitching pair of splendid haunches, to a moist, hot orifice which opens up for him and takes hold of him and squeezes him, like a ripe fruit. Elia has been elevated or degraded to her final, essential, undeniable character — that of the female in the springtime.

Elia wakes up to find Ricardo's mouth touching her cheek, and his hand, gentle and timid now, on her naked breast under the sheet. "I've got to go now," he says. "How do you feel? You're not cross, are you?" She wakes up with a vivid, unmistakable sensation of discomfort, with the unambiguous feeling that something has gone very wrong. This sensation of fear, anxiety and grief often attacks her at the moment of waking and it's generally several seconds before she can remember the causes of her sadness, fear or discomfort; but this time memory returns at once, with a stabbing immediacy. "What about Clara? Where's Clara?" she cries, as a giddying series of images unrolls before her: Clara smoking hashish like a good, diligent little girl; Clara drinking champagne though she doesn't like it; Clara's astonished and desolate eyes searching for Elia's with a puzzled, questioning look, which is the terrible look we see in the eyes of children and animals who suffer without understanding why, while Ricardo drugs her, undresses her, mauls her and makes her get into bed. (Elia sees all this happen out of the corner of her eye, although she pretends to concentrate on the exact folding of the coverlet.) The series of images continues: Clara in Elia's arms, trembling, vulnerable and warm, trying so pathetically hard to hold back her tears, and even to make a little joke, while Elia persists in pretending not to understand; Clara struggling at her side in the octopus grasp of Ricardo's legs and arms, overcome by disgust and terror, while Elia takes such a long time to make up her mind to invervene and get Clara away from him; Clara jerking her head desperately from side to side on the pillow, her thighs braced, her knees trembling but held tightly together; Clara sobbing as she is pushed to one side, left on the edge of the group, although she still probably can't help watching them, while Ricardo rides on top of Elia like a madman; the young poet that Elia loved not long ago for his diffidence, for his timidity and for his inexperience has become the most arrogant and greedy of the great apes. Attached to the end of this chain of images is one which can't be a memory; it's more of a premonition, or a crazy fantasy, a projection of Elia's apprehensions and her bad conscience. If it had really happened, she would have heard a disturbance in the street below the terrace, and Ricardo wouldn't still be lying here, perfectly calm except for a touch of embarrassed contrition (not unmixed with vanity), like a child who has

136

done something slightly naughty, with his hand resting casually on her breast as it might rest on the handlebars of a bicycle or the head of a dog that belonged to him . . . No, it must have been a delusion produced by Elia's feelings of guilt and fear, that terrible picture of Clara, so much more horrible than all the other images that are definitely memories — that picture of Clara climbing naked on to the stone balustrade at the edge of the terrace, between the gardenias in their pots and the silent, terrified canaries in their cages, and of Clara jumping out into space with a terrifying scream, or a still more terrible silence, or with the rasping yowl of a cat falling into the void while trying to escape some danger. Equally unreal is the other picture of Clara walking along the street beneath the fresh green branches of the sleeping trees, keeping close to the walls as if tormented by fear or by cold, cat-like in this too — like the cats that Elia has sometimes seen foraging around the doors of the street where Clara lives (but never in the residential part of the city), keeping close to the walls like a cat who has been irrevocably expelled from paradise, with the finality that goes with loss of faith. There can be no doubt that Clara has now lost her belief in the paradise of the cats, although she probably still believes in hell — not the hell which awaits her in the hereafter, beyond the fragile veil of death, but the hell of the stray cats who have lost their faith and abandoned all hope and, worse still, all desire of finding that impossible paradise, sunk in that total void where even desire is dead. That's the hell that Clara must be exploring now, thinks Elia, as she slinks furtively along, very close to the house-fronts, crossing the road without paying any heed to the traffic lights or to the blaring horns of approaching cars, none of which will ever now turn out to be the carriage of the Queen of the Cats; pausing in a doorway from time to time to swallow a round, pink sleeping pill, not taking them all at once, but swallowing them with pleasurable anguish one after another. At this point Elia pushes Ricardo's lips away from her cheek and his hand away from her breast, and sits up. She turns on the light and looks in the drawer of the bedside table. The medicine bottle is there, with all the sleeping pills inside it. Ricardo looks at her apprehensively, slightly alarmed, perhaps afraid that the naughtiness has gone too far and might produce some unforeseen misfortune, like a child looking at his parents to see whether he's going to be scolded, forgiven or punished. There's no trace of the ape from the jungle, no trace of the dominant, possessive male; he has recovered some of the ambiguous charm of his former timid uncertainty. "What's wrong?" he asks. "Clara went away a long time ago; you've been asleep for more than two hours, Elia." Then he seems to guess what is in her mind. "Don't worry; nobody dies of love," he says with a smile. "Nobody kills themselves for love." Strange that it should be the poet who says this; but he's right. No one, not even Clara, kills themselves for love; there was no scream from outside the window, no naked body falling from the terrace before the fascinated, horrified eyes of a group of passers-by; and here are all the pink pills in their little bottle of coloured glass. Nobody, not even Clara, dies or kills themselves for love. Elia sighs, not sure whether she's relieved or disappointed, and assures Ricardo that nothing has changed, that he can go home with his mind at rest, that she just hadn't realised how late it was. It's quite dark outside and the birds have stopped singing while she's been asleep. She tells Ricardo that she's all right, that she loves him as much as ever, that they'll meet again tomorrow. No longer ape-like, the poet looks supplicatingly at her, his virginity miraculously restored by his fear of losing her, his fear that Elia might abandon him. His hand is on her breast again, and he begins to finger her nipple with a series of repeated, mechanical, nervous

138

caresses of a kind which always irritates her, unbearably, and which now make her even more anxious to get rid of him, impatient to see him go, so that she nervously repeats her protestations and reassurances until Ricardo's mind is at rest. He gives her a goodbye kiss and finally — at last — gets out of the bedroom and out of the house.

A few seconds later, Elia hears the sound of paws crossing the floor, and Muslina quietly jumps up on to the bed and settles back into her rightful place, now that the intruder has gone. The cat's green, dilated eyes look into Elia's from a distance of a few inches, observing her doubtfully. She sniffs at Elia's mouth, nipples and belly, and her sense of smell probably tells her exactly what has been going on. Muslina scowls and snorts in disgust at the smell of the intruder, a bitter smell of sweat and sex, of the beast hidden in the cave; but then she stretches out, resigned or indulgent, and lies down at Elia's side in her usual way, lengthwise against her body, with as much skin-to-skin contact as possible, and stays there motionless, pressed up against Elia as she always does, reflecting that the proper order of things has now been re-established, with everything back in its right place, the only disturbing factor being that penetrating, unfriendly, unfamiliar smell.

Well, thinks Elia, it's quite certain that Clara hasn't jumped over the edge of the terrace, nor swallowed a series of pink sleeping-pills in the friendly obscurity of the doorways and porches of the city streets. But does this thought inspire her with relief or disappointment? — or rather does relief or disappointment play the larger role in her confused and ambivalent feelings? And another thing that's quite certain, thinks Elia, is that in a few minutes time, when she's had a shower and made herself a nice cup of tea, and closed the windows to keep out the night air, she'll begin trying to get Clara on the telephone. And sooner or later, Clara will

swallow down the worst of her bitterness and disenchantment, as she wanders through the avenues and streets and
squares of the city, and will turn homeward. Still ignoring
traffic lights and blaring motor horns, but not getting hurt
as a result, she will make her way home, through streets that
become narrower and treeless as she gets nearer her
destination; and then it's certain that she'll be there to answer
the telephone. Her voice will be a little husky, very sad, and
perhaps a trifle disgusted; but she will answer in the end. Elia
will try to pacify and console her, will try above all to assure
herself that she has not lost Clara, that what has happened is
just a piece of childish naughtiness, which must have already
been forgiven on that basis; the words Elia uses to Clara will
owe a good deal to those uttered by Ricardo a few minutes
ago. Elia will tell Clara again and again over the telephone, as
often as is necessary, that nothing really happened in the flat
today, that nothing happened at all. She'll tell Clara —
without knowing whether she is speaking the truth or not —
that Ricardo is just an episode, one adventure more in her life
as an idle, unsatisfied, bored woman — one of those things
that you let yourself in for without really wanting to, because
you can't help it; it's just an adventure which may last a few
more weeks or months, whereas the friendship between two
women, between Clara and herself, operates at a deeper level
and will last a whole lifetime. And in the end Clara will
believe her or pretend to believe her, and give in and promise
to come and see her tomorrow. And why shouldn't Elia's flat
still be that improbable but necessary paradise, the fasci-
nating paradise of the cats? And so tomorrow the three of
them will again take up the threads of their game — though it
may be a bit more than a game for Clara, even if she isn't
capable of dying of love or killing herself for love — all three
of them involved, or rather ensnared, in a match against
themselves or against the devil, as the case may be, because

a game like this can come to an end only when the players cease to find any sort of reward or pleasure in it, only when there is not a single counter left on the board. For the duration of this long summer in the city, with its sticky heat, dust and emptiness, this interminable summer that has scarcely begun, Elia cannot or will not give up anything, no matter how sordid or trivial it may be, which can free her even temporarily from her boredom and depression, from her panic fear of old age and death. She cannot give up anything which may postpone the moment when she must again confront her unrecognisable image in a mirror, in the eyes of her husband, her sons or her lovers — that implacable image, which now seems to have been magically abolished and replaced by another image, impermanent but at least quite different from the first. This second image may have originated in a dream of her own; but she finds it again, enlarged, three-dimensional and almost wholly convincing, in the eyes of the two young people who have reinvented it.

Ricardo, too, cannot and will not abandon the game at present, for a number of reasons. He needs to prove some things to himself — the power of his will, the strength of his intelligence, perhaps his possession of creative genius — by means of this system of composing real-life stories, with characters of flesh and blood; a pretty story in this case, a trivial little story with three characters. He passionately needs an outlet for the thronging fantasies of his childhood and adolescence. And then there's his delusion that in Elia he has found not merely a source of immediate pleasure but a launching-pad from which he can take off for the conquest of other women, if not the conquest of the world. There's a lot of ambition and selfishness in these timid, frightened, humiliated boys, thinks Elia.

And then there's Clara, the young girl in love, the one positively good character in this episode, which hardly qualifies to be called a story — Clara who created the title of Queen of the Cats for Elia out of the kindness of her loving heart, who has said "Be it done unto me in accordance with your word" and "My loneliness begins six feet from where you stand," whose huge, astonished eyes reflect the best possible or impossible image of Elia. Even Clara cannot and will not abandon the game before it reaches its end, because, to Elia's amazement she loves her. Whatever can this crazy child have seen in me? wonders Elia. Clara therefore has the largest share both of suffering and of happiness. At the end of the day, concludes Elia, whose feelings of guilt dwindle and vanish at this point, it's Clara who has the best of it; it's Clara who has landed the most brilliant and attractive role in the farce. And so the three of them will stay together, sometimes making each other happy and sometimes hurting each other, until the magic circle is broken and the game comes to an end, without a single counter left on the table and without a single card left to play. Then Clara and Ricardo will vanish out of Elia's life to break new ground somewhere else — both of them are, after all, so terrifyingly young — and Elia will sink into another abyss of boredom and discontent, with Muslina or some successor of Muslina at her side, swallowed up again by the round of doctors and travels for the good of her health and rest cures and convalescence and plans to study something or take up a job. There will be a period of weeks or months during which her melancholy figure can be seen in society, appearing zombie-like at the opening of exhibitions, at first nights, at concerts, at friends' houses, until finally she collapses again and starts spending hour after empty hour in bed, or in front of the television, now gazing unseeingly at the mouldings of the ceiling, the pictures on the walls and the images that appear on the screen, and now lying with her face to the wall or sitting with her head held in her hands, too listless to light a cigarette, put on a record, say a word to the

142

children, or answer the telephone when a friend rings her up. It's worse than being dead, much worse than being dead, and the only thing that keeps her going, the only stimulus that makes her continue the masquerade and stay alive, is the hope that even now something will come into her life from outside and set her in motion again, making her flower as the desert cactus flowers after an agony of drought, and bringing back, for another brief period, the illusion of existing through the existence of others, of feeling oneself alive through the feelings of others . . . until finally, some day, all miracles cease and the whole dismal, pointless, dirty, solitary story reaches its ultimate happy ending.